St. Johns Wood

From Waverly Fitzgerald

Fiction
St. John's Wood
Chelsea
Mayfair
Grover Square

As Waverly Curtis
co-authored with Curt Colbert
Dial C for Chihuahua
Chihuahua Confidential
The Big Chihuahua
The Chihuahua Always Sniffs Twice
A Chihuahua in Every Stocking

Nonfiction
Slow Time: Recovering the Natural Rhythm of Life

St. Johns Wood

Waverly Fitzgerald

GENESTA PRESS

First published in hardcover in 1977 by Doubleday & Company, Inc.
First published in paperback in 1977 by Popular Library
This edition published in 2018 by Genesta Press.

ISBN 978-0-9835714-4-5
Library of Congress Catalog Card Number 76-42326

Genesta Press
1211 E Denny Way #187
Seattle WA U.S.A. 98112

For Gene and Ellen

Contents

St. Johns Wood

Chapter One

In Which the Reader Makes the Acquaintance of Miss Thalia Horrocks

"MISS MALLET," THALIA SAID, "be good enough to play for us that charming Beethoven sonata you have begun teaching me. I feel sure that Letty would enjoy it."

The elderly lady flushed and rose awkwardly from her chair to cross to the far side of the drawing room and seat herself at the piano. She was not an accomplished musician; her sole criterion for excellence was volume. But as she began her crashing and discordant interpretation of the piece which had been requested, Thalia smiled, for she had created this diversion deliberately. Glancing at her younger sister and observing that Flora was very much absorbed in the portfolio of drawings which she was examining, Thalia moved closer to her cousin Letitia and whispered violently, "Letty, where is Lynton? I must see him."

Letty looked up from her embroidery with a puzzled frown.

"Thalia," she said clearly, struggling to raise her voice over the dissonant tones of the piano, "you must speak more distinctly. I assure you I cannot understand a word you say."

Exasperated, Thalia replied urgently, "Letty, that is exactly my purpose. I am trying to divert the attention of Miss Mallet and

Flora so that I may discover the whereabouts of your brother
Lynton."

"My brother—Lynton," repeated Letty in a confused manner.
Prevarication was as alien to her nature as intrigue was natural to
Thalia's. "But why, Thalia dear, do you wish to see Lynton, and so
immediately?"

Thalia glanced around the room again to observe that Miss
Mallet was still absorbed in her sonata and her younger sister still
immersed in her study of the drawings.

"Letty," she whispered, "you cannot imagine the smashing
Scheme I have invented." Her eyes sparkled with excitement. "But
it requires the aid of Lynton. I will reveal it completely to you as
soon as I have discussed it with him. But where is he?"

Letty took a moment to digest this information. A thousand
questions and cautions passed through her mind, but from long
experience she knew it would be useless to halt her cousin in the
midst of one of her adventures. With a sigh, she resumed her
needlework and said patiently, "Lynton is usually riding in the Park
in the afternoon, in Rotten Row, with several of his friends."

On this occasion, it was Thalia who could not hear, as Miss
Mallet had reached the thundering finale of her piece. Letty was
forced to repeat herself several times and, as Miss Mallet crashed
down upon the keys in one final reverberating chord, her words
rang out clearly in the subsequent silence:

"He's to be found in Rotten Row."

Flora looked up sharply. She was very jealous of her older
sister and realized instinctively that something was afoot which
she could perhaps turn to her advantage.

"Who is in the Park, Letty?" she inquired quickly.

"Oh, it's of no consequence," Thalia interrupted, trying to hide
Letty's confusion and her desire to reveal the truth. "Merely one of
Letty's acquaintances—she met him at the ball at Lady Calverly's
house last week, the son of one of the Viscountess's dear friends.
He is a capable horseman, and Letty was saying that he spends
much of his time riding in the Park."

Letty looked at Thalia reproachfully with her large grey eyes
but did not deny this elaborate fabrication.

Miss Mallet had risen from the piano, perplexed as to what was being discussed at the other end of the room, and, as she approached the three girls, Thalia jumped up and announced imperatively,

"We really must be leaving. Letty was just remarking that she was quite fatigued and desired to rest before she dresses for the dinner at the Beverwills' tonight."

Letty shot Thalia another mournful look and sighed, but Thalia smiled irrepressibly and bent to kiss her.

"Thank you awfully, coz. You're a dear."

Miss Mallet frowned, appalled at the slang which Thalia was using, but she forbore to correct her ward, as she was intimidated by the grandeur of the house at which they were calling. However her sense of duty was strong and as soon as she and Thalia and Flora were ensconced in their closed brougham and were driving slowly through the crowded London streets, she delivered her customary lecture upon the impropriety of the use of slang by young ladies.

By the time they had reached Russell Square, Thalia seemed subdued and chastened by her governess's remonstrances, but she bounded out of the brougham in a very unladylike manner, her crinoline flying up to reveal her white-stockinged legs to the world (which consisted merely of the elderly coachman, Joseph), and was running into the house before Miss Mallet could utter a reproof.

Thalia clattered up the stairs to her bedroom and slammed the door shut, not quite deliberately but not entirely innocently either. She undid the many buttons and bows of her new lilac-and-cherry-striped morning dress carelessly and, tossing it on a nearby footstool, rummaged through the wardrobe for her riding habit. She was particularly fond of this garment, as she knew that the deep brown colour suited her and the close fit displayed to admiration her neat figure. Unfortunately, it was very old-fashioned. Thalia knew that next to the bejewelled and gaudily dressed women who acquired their livelihood by driving in the Park she would look a dowd. Yet there was no hope that her mother would permit her to leave the house in the type of ravishing costume which she envisioned. Therefore she pulled on her boots and crammed the old straw hat garnished with artificial flowers onto her dark curls without a glance at the mirror and left the room abruptly, encountering Miss Mallet and Flora sedately ascending the stairs, one before the other because of the width of their crinolines.

"Why, Miss Thalia," gasped the elderly governess, "what are you doing? Where are you going?"

"I am going riding," Thalia replied innocently, "and so shall you as soon as you put on your riding habit. Do hurry, Mallie, before the sun disappears."

The governess blinked her eyes a few times and then went to do as Thalia had asked. She was a very biddable woman. Thalia had been able to manage her since the day she had arrived in the Horrocks household ten years before.

This brief altercation had brought Thalia's mother, Mrs. Horrocks, from her downstairs sitting room, and she stood at the foot of the stairs remarking sharply, "Thalia, what is the meaning of this disgraceful conduct—slamming of doors and shouting on the stairwell? Come down here immediately and explain to me, in a fashion suitable to a lady, the reason for this disturbance."

Flora, who had remained halfway up the stairs for this entire period of time and was indeed blocking Thalia's way with the width of her skirts, said petulantly, "Mama, Thalia is going to meet a young man in the Park, a friend of Letty's. They were talking of him together."

"We will discuss this in the appropriate manner in the sitting room," Mrs. Horrocks replied grimly. "I wish you both to attend me there." Nonplussed at the turn of events occasioned by her story of Letty's imaginary young man, Thalia followed her sister downstairs and into the sitting room.

This room was furnished entirely to Mrs. Horrocks' taste and exactly contrary to Thalia's likes. It was a jungle of small tables cluttered with pottery, porcelain statues, and glass knickknacks, and dotted with small, fragile-looking *papier-maché* chairs inlaid with scenes of the Crystal Palace from the Great Exhibition and portraits of the Queen and the Prince Consort. Engraved depictions of the Progress of Civilization hung upon the walls and almost obscured the patterned purple wallpaper but unfortunately (in Thalia's mind) did not succeed entirely in doing so. There was always little light in the room, for the heavy purple velvet draperies prevented the entrance of all but the most daring sunbeams, and thus the room was immured in a perpetual twilight. Thalia had more of a horror of this room than of any other in the house; the clutter, confounded with the closeness of the air, acted upon her as a soporific. She fell onto a nearby chair.

"Thalia," Mrs. Horrocks said with a cold tone in her voice, "a lady seats herself upon a chair. She does not fall upon it. Rise and seat yourself properly."

Thalia did as she was told. To argue was useless. Her usually quick mind could not even contrive a story suitable for explaining her desire to ride in the Park. By the time her mother had finished questioning Flora and turned to Thalia, she could only say lamely that she did not know even the name of the young man to whom Letty had referred, that she merely desired to ride before luncheon, as she enjoyed riding and that Miss Mallet would accompany her to prevent her from forming any unsuitable friendships. This entire speech seemed paltry to Thalia, and her voice trailed away at the end, particularly since Miss Mallet had wandered into the room in her faded and old-fashioned grey riding habit and was wringing her hands helplessly, as altercations upset her. She seemed more in need of protection than Thalia herself.

Mrs. Horrocks, seated at her writing desk, held her hand over her eyes for a few moments and thought. Her eldest daughter was her greatest trial. She was noisy; she was boisterous; she was always involved in escapades of the most shocking nature. She was disrespectful and disobedient to her parents, bold and impertinent, and heedless of the dangers incurred to her own reputation. She was even irreligious, for Mrs. Horrocks had once found her reading a Sentimental Novel within the covers of her Bible on a Sunday. And yet, it would certainly be a great relief to have her out of the house, if only for an hour. Mrs. Horrocks was enduring one of her monthly headaches with grim and silent fortitude. Her own pain was not sufficient reason to permit her daughter to escape her rigid surveillance, but her need for peace conquered her strict moral precepts.

She turned to the governess and said irritably, "Miss Mallet, I entrust you with the grave and difficult responsibility of watching over my eldest daughter. You are to accompany her to the Park; you are not to leave her side for a moment. You remember that just last week while she was supposed to be practicing on the piano she left the house quite unaccompanied and rode in the Park alone." Mrs. Horrocks shuddered. "If any one of our acquaintance had seen her there she would be lost. She would be condemned to a life of spinsterhood." Miss Mallet coloured slightly but the others did not notice her. "If she is not, indeed, condemned to it already," continued Mrs. Horrocks, "for with her bold manners and in-elegant speech I cannot imagine any fine young man, such as Frederic Cornfield, wishing to offer for her." She rattled on with further examples of Thalia's misconduct, speaking of her daughter as she often did in this third-hand manner. Thalia in fact had listened to none of this speech, having heard the whole of it before. She waited until her mother had dismissed them all and then exited quickly, ignoring Mrs. Horrocks' last demand that she pin back the curls that were straying from under her hat.

Thalia had quite recovered her spirits by the time she and Miss Mallet had mounted their horses and were riding to the Park. It was an unusually sunny day in late June, without a hint of cloud in the blue sky, and at the Height of the Season. The ordinarily crowded streets were filled to capacity with exceptionally heavy traffic, for on such a fine day most of fashionable London headed for the rendezvous of the Park.

Thalia, engrossed in planning the details of her latest scheme, had unthinkingly allowed Miss Mallet to lead the way and was brought up sharply from her reveries by the unpleasant realization that they were in the centre of a horrendous traffic jam on Oxford Street. The entire length of the thoroughfare was filled from side to side with every type of vehicle: ponderous family carriages, light phaetons with well-dressed young swells at the ribbons chafing at the impediments in their path, hackney coaches with the drivers swearing volubly at the swinish nature of all those who had chosen to travel via Oxford Street that morning. Taking advantage of the captive occupants of the carriages and landaus were the street vendors, who wove their way in and out of the fretting horses and curious pedestrians, poking their heads into carriage windows and crying their wares. The Italian ice man was doing a good business, as was the bearward on the corner, who had gathered a large crowd with the antics of his huge, shabby-looking animal friend. Thalia watched the bear's performance for a moment; he had once been a beautiful, proud animal; she was struck by the nobility of his large dark eyes. But in the heat of the summer his hair had become patchy and the iron collar about his neck, attached to a heavy chain which ran to his master's belt, had rubbed away the fur underneath. Even from her position several yards away, Thalia could see that the skin there was sore and probably infected. Although the bear continued to gyrate pleasantly, almost unbalancing himself and gesticulating mildly with his paws, she turned away in disgust. There was a kinship, she thought for a moment, between herself and the captive animal. She too was bound, by the iron collar of Gentility, to her mama, who forced her to dance politely and murmur the correct social pleasantries in the hopes that Thalia would attract the riches of some enterprising young man.

"Miss Mallet," Thalia said, reaching over and taking hold of the bridle of her governess' horse, "it would be wiser to journey down one of the smaller streets."

By way of assent, Miss Mallet bobbed her head up and down several times in rapid succession, and Thalia forcefully cleared a path to one of the smaller roads opening off Oxford Street. It required much determination: hackney coachmen swore at the impertinent young girl; several of the young swells at the ribbons of their phaetons glanced at her suggestively, taking in the curve of her breasts under the tightly buttoned bodice of the habit and the smallness of her waist where the heavy overskirt fastened. Thalia ignored these comments and looks resolutely, and soon she and Miss Mallet were headed down a smaller street, almost a back alley, towards the Park.

Miss Mallet, uncomfortable in the press of traffic on Oxford Street, was yet more ill at ease in their new surroundings. The small, dingy houses bore a secretive look; at this hour, when even the most indolent of the upper classes had risen for breakfast, the blinds were still drawn. Servant girls, who should have been inside scrubbing the kitchen and cleaning the bedrooms, were lounging on the area railings, flirting with the tradesmen's boys delivering goods. The humbler street vendors who haunted residential areas were wandering up and down calling their wares.

"Milk-o, Milk-o!" shouted the milkman; "Old clo'," a very aged old-clothes man grunted in chorus.

A bent old woman in shabby clothes and a rusty cloak, bearing on her back a bundle of freshly made birch brooms, screamed "Fine brooms, fine brooms, only one penny," in a shrill, quavering voice, but there was no response from any of the strangely slumbering houses, and the maids merely ignored the vendors or made them the object of jokes told to the tradesmen's boys, who raised shouts of raucous laughter.

Fortunately for Miss Mallet, this thoroughfare was swifter than Oxford Street, and she and Thalia soon emerged at the Marble Arch corner of the Park and began to make their way towards Rotten Row to the south. The Park during the Season resembled a large open drawing room. Families in huge carriages, pretty young women in open victorias and sociables, all paused in their sedate progress down the crowded drives of the Park to greet old friends and carry on protracted conversations heedless of the standstill of traffic behind them. Thalia, who ordinarily enjoyed the pageantry of this scene and liked to take in the details of the fashionable costumes, was annoyed today, for her main object was to search out Lynton Lanston as quickly as possible. As usual, there were few persons there of her acquaintance—merely one or two of Letitia's friends whom she had met at the Lanston house, and therefore she was not obliged to pause to acknowledge anyone.

She began, quite uncivilly, to prod her mount, a good-natured but massive bay, into the smallest openings in the traffic jam, and then by propelling him forward, force her way between the clusters of people and horses. Miss Mallet was an unwilling shadow in this pursuit. Upon her fell the opprobrium of those who had been jostled by Thalia's tactics, and she rode meekly, her eyes cast down so as to avoid their angry glances.

It was in this manner that she suddenly lost sight of Thalia. One moment the slim figure in the brown habit had been there before her, driving a wedge into yet another conversation; the next moment Miss Mallet looked up to find that Thalia had vanished, as if into thin air, and she herself was in the middle of a ring of people, whose exchange of gossip she had interrupted. They glared at her maliciously, and Miss Mallet searched desperately for some gap in the circle of horses and riders through which she could exit. When this gap finally appeared and she had made her escape, Thalia was nowhere in sight. The only recourse was to follow in the direction she had been heading; however, since Miss Mallet was not as intrepid a horsewoman as Thalia, her progress was infinitely slow and she was frequently boxed into a corner and forced to listen to the chatter of those beside her.

Thalia had known instantly the moment she had lost Miss Mallet; she experienced with a sense of relief the absence of that anxious gaze fixed upon the small of her back. She had intended to leave Miss Mallet behind eventually; it was perhaps better that it had happened so soon for she could move much faster, un-impeded by the necessity of pushing a way for two horses between the crowds, especially as Miss Mallet was so timid that she often let a gap that Thalia had opened close before her. She was unperturbed by the fact that she was riding in the Park without an escort, an adventure that had compromised many a young girl and an older woman who had done so before her. She could not credit that among so many people any one would be able to perceive that she was unaccompanied. Why, her escort might have been any of the grooms or formidable mothers accompanying the other riders in the Park, from which for a moment she had been irrevocably parted.

With a new sense of freedom and excitement, she made her way down the crowded pathways and onto Rotten Row. As she neared the Achilles statue, where Skittles, the Queen of the London "pretty horsebreakers," held court for the young men of Belgravia and Mayfair, Thalia spotted Lynton and made her way towards him.

He was with a group of young swells standing about the bright blue phaeton of an exceptionally pretty young girl, who was dressed in a bright blue gown and flanked by two little pages in livery of the same shade. She wore a fashionable pork-pie hat over her blond ringlets and its blue feather dipped and swayed as she coquetted with her head in response to the remarks of the gentlemen. Lynton, suddenly glancing up to see Thalia riding towards him, disconnected himself from this group and moved towards her, taking hold of her horse's bridle and pulling her over towards the side of the pathway.

"Thalia, good God, what are you doing here? Where is your companion?" he inquired abruptly, glancing around to see if he could espy such a person.

"I unfortunately lost her, back there somewhere," Thalia said with a pretty sigh, waving her hand in the general direction of the rest of the Park. "And so knowing that you would be here, I came to find you and beg your protection."

Lynton looked up sharply at his cousin, but perceiving the roguish smile upon her face, immediately discerned that this was not the truth.

"Thalia," he said pompously, "I have told you repeatedly that you are a minx. If I were your brother I should lock you up in the coal cellar until you promised to reform."

Thalia ignored this gallant comment and instead glanced across at the elegant young lady in blue.

"Pray, who is she, Lynton?" she inquired with a tone of assumed innocence.

"Thalia, you know damned well," Lynton began, and then choked back his words. "Dash it all, you irritate me so I begin to swear in front of you—she is merely an acquaintance."

"May I be introduced to her?" Thalia continued ingenuously.

"Certainly not," Lynton responded with an air of finality. "If you have nothing better to discuss, I will return you immediately to the care of your companion. I assume it is the admirable Miss Mallet. Where is she?"

"I do not know, Lynton," answered Thalia, dropping her bantering tone and leaning down to speak more discreetly.

"Lynton, before we find her, or she finds us, there is something quite serious which I must discuss with you."

"Then you must dismount. We cannot carry on an important conversation in this manner," said Lynton, offering his hand so that she could step down from her horse, which she did gracefully. The long skirt of her riding habit trailed in the dust, and Thalia, gathering it up, stooped under the wooden barrier that lined the pathway and tied the horse's reins to it. Then she and Lynton moved into the shade of a nearby tree.

"Lynton," Thalia announced importantly, as soon as they were out of the hearing range of the other Parkgoers, "I am going to write a Novel."

Lynton, who was not at all literary, shrugged his shoulders.

"A Novel," Thalia continued, "in the style of Ouida. And my subject will be the pretty horsebreakers."

This brought a reaction from her cousin.

"Thalia, you cannot," he sputtered.

"And why not?" she inquired, wide-eyed.

A thousand objections passed through Lynton's thoughts, but the first which he could grasp and frame into suitable words was an aphorism he remembered his tutor relating to him;

"Because writers should only write about subjects they know first-hand," he said with great dignity.

"Exactly, Lynton," exclaimed Thalia, bouncing up and down. "I am surprised you came so quickly to the point. I wish you to introduce me to several of the 'pretty horse-breakers' of your acquaintance in order that I may interview them and discover their feelings about their way of life." She waved her hands towards the Achilles statue. "Especially the 'fair Anonyma,'" she said, referring to Skittles. "Can you introduce me to her, Lynton?"

Lynton was at a loss for words again. "Of course I cannot introduce you," he stammered. "Why, she uses language no disreputable coachman would use before a young miss such as yourself." He frowned. "How do you know about Skittles, and where did you learn the phrase 'pretty horsebreakers' ?"

"From *The Times*," Thalia said. "Of course my stepfather does not allow us to read it; after he has finished with it in the morning

11

he gives it to Betty to burn. But I have made special arrangements with her. I give her the novels from Mudie's which your sister lends to me, and in return, she rescues *The Times* from the fire. Every morning when I awake it is by my bedside and I read it over thoroughly before going down to breakfast." She smiled ingenuously. "In fact, Lynton, I know about the most shocking things."

Lynton had no doubt that she did. The London *Times* was filled with the sordid details of every important Society Divorce case, as well as numerous letters about that segment of female society formerly known as the Cyprians, but now referred to as the "pretty horsebreakers" since their takeover of the Park as a gathering place. Foremost among them was Skittles, or, as *The Times* had christened her, 'the fair Anonyma.' She had appeared one day in the past year, charmingly dressed and controlling superbly a beautiful and spirited matched pair; the rumour was that she had been hired by the owner of a livery stables to display his animals in the Park. Now the thoroughfare from Knightsbridge to Apsley House, which had formerly been deserted, was lined with curious sightseers who set up chairs along the sides of the road to watch for the approach of Skittles.

"I must say, Thalia," her cousin remarked sternly, "that you are indeed not at all a respectable young miss. One might even label you 'fast.'"

"One might," said Thalia demurely. "But you have not yet answered my question. If not Skittles, wouldn't you introduce me to another horsebreaker, perhaps a semi-respectable one who does not use shocking language?"

"There is none such," muttered Lynton, and then more loudly, although with a note of uncertainty, "absolutely not. I will not be a party to this disgraceful scheme of yours."

Thalia broke into a torrent of speech at this refusal. "Lynton, you do not understand what this means to me. I must write a novel and it must be about the pretty horsebreakers; for in that manner I will make a great deal of money which I will use to rent a little house in some part of London, or the country, it matters little where, and live there by myself or perhaps with Miss Mallet. I can no longer bear my life as it is now. My mama is always watching me as if I were a prisoner and she my jailer. And Mr. Horrocks, you know, my stepfather, is a cruel man; if he finds that I have given Mama the slightest twinge of pain, and you know I often do that—although I don't in the least intend it—he locks me into my room for days on end, allowing no one to speak to me or even attend me. He has Cook bring up buttered bread and tea and leave it outside the door. Then he unlocks it himself and stands over me silently while I am eating, almost as if he fears I will somehow contrive to fashion the teaspoon into a tool which I can use to effect an escape. I once attempted to escape by tying my sheets together, as one reads about in novels, but when I had let them out of my window, I discovered that I could not fit through, for the window is too small. Only a fortnight ago I was locked into my room for two days and given a Bible to read so that I could repent of my evil deeds, and do you know, Lynton, what I had done?"

She went on without expecting an answer. "I refused to play the piano before company which we had one night. But I only refused because I know I am a terrible player. And I did perform the piece, after protesting, although I must admit I did not take much care with it and made more than five or six mistakes each minute. They said they were angry with me because I had been disobedient, but in fact it was because our guests were Mr. and Mrs. Cornfield and their toadlike son Frederic, whom they wish me to marry. And I assure you, Lynton, that marriage to him would be a fate worse than death!"

Thalia could see that this dramatic speech had not in the least affected her cousin; he merely smiled at this account of her latest misbehaviour.

"Lynton!" she cried desperately. "You must understand the tedium of my day-to-day existence. I arise near dawn each morning, for Mama requires it of us, though no one else in the whole of London rises until many hours later—except, of course, the servants. We breakfast and then she expects me to spend the remaining hours of the day either practicing the piano (which I detest) or embroidering (which I loathe). She never permits us to go out on calls, unless she accompanies us, and then only to the

13

houses of her friends. Your sister Letty is the sole exception, for reasons which you know, but Mama often refuses to let me visit her, as she says I do so too often. When my stepfather returns home at the close of the day from the City, we have an early dinner, at which we are not allowed to speak unless directly questioned, and then he reads to us from the Bible for hours on end. By ten o'clock we must be in bed, although on Saturdays it is a little later, for Mama forces us to take a bath. Lynton, I implore you, could you support such an existence? I warn you that if you do not help me I must do something desperate."

She ended this speech in a tone of defiance and glared at her cousin with her large, dark eyes.

Lynton, unmoved by Thalia's recounting of what seemed to him mere childish pranks, was much affected by the last part of her speech. The hours which she kept were shocking; her parents seemed to him monsters. His sister Letitia, he knew, kept the hours of fashionable London, arising close to noon, calling upon friends until teatime, then returning home to dress for dinner, which was taken either at the home of friends or in a large company at the family mansion on Mount Street. After dining, Letty began the long round of parties and routs and balls, often leaving one house at three to go to a cotillion which was just beginning at another, and returning home as the sun was rising. He was horrified at the thought of parents who did not permit their daughter to go out on calls except to the homes of their stuffy friends, and who forced her to take, indignity of all indignities, a bath once a week.

Lynton had offered a superficial resistance to the idea of a well-bred young girl being exposed to the society of the muslin company, but in truth he felt disinclined to pursue this objection. He was a fast young man: bred, as Mrs. Horrocks would have said, to indolence and dissolution. His father, the Viscount, simply considered that his son was sowing his wild oats, a perfectly reasonable pastime for a young aristocrat; but his mother, the Viscountess, sensed that his irresponsible behaviour was more deeply rooted. She feared that aside from a surface acquaintanceship, he had no real understanding of social conventions, and that he would continue through life as he had begun, making no distinctions whatsoever between the proper and the improper forms of behaviour. The paltry objections which he had offered to Thalia were all that his mother had been able to breed into him, but after several minutes of prolonged concentration Lynton could uncover no real excuse for refusing to help his cousin. In any event, her story had deeply affected him; he wished to aid her and he thought that the entire proposal could have few adverse repercussions upon him.

Thalia immediately sensed his encouraging response and flung her arms around him. "Oh, thank you, Lynton!" she cried. "You can pretend that I am one of your lady friends. It will be the greatest fun imaginable. And furthermore I will dedicate my book to you."

She began to dance about with her arms still clasped around his waist. Lynton, after reviewing his thoughts and considering that he had made the right decision, smiled at her enthusiasm and, putting his arms about her waist, tossed her high into the air.

Hampered by the overly long skirts of her riding habit, Thalia lost her footing as she descended and fell backwards upon the ground. Bending to help extricate her from this awkward position, Lynton frowned again.

"Now what is amiss?" Thalia asked impatiently, brushing the twigs and leaves from her skirt.

"You certainly could not pass as one of my lady friends wearing the type of clothes you usually wear," replied Lynton quite callously. "Have you anything a bit more dashing?"

"Of course I do not," Thalia said, understandably annoyed, for one of her chief desires was to be in possession of a huge wardrobe filled with ravishing costumes. "Mama refuses to allow me to choose my own clothes. She says that if I did I would make a spectacle of myself." She paused a moment; then her eyes brightened. "But perhaps I could borrow a dress from Letty. I am sure she would be glad to loan me anything and we are about the same size. I will call upon her tomorrow and find something. You need not be ashamed of me, Lynton."

Her cousin was not at all reassured by this as he considered that his sister was second only to Thalia in the dowdiness of her clothes. While Thalia was usually dressed in the shockingly vulgar orange-and-purple-striped costumes which her mother loved, his sister Letty, although she was dressed by one of the most fashionable dressmakers in London, preferred dove grey and soft brown dresses with a conspicuous lack of ornament. Hoping, but without much real faith, that something could be concocted by combining Thalia's extravagant tastes and his sister's expensive wardrobe, he decided to leave the matter entirely to the female mind which was better equipped to deal with the intricacies of fashion than his own.

At this moment, the desperate Miss Mallet appeared, almost driving her horse through the barrier in her attempt to reach her ward and shrieking "Thalia! Thalia!" in a shrill, loud voice.

All those in the immediate vicinity turned to watch the interesting scene about to be enacted as Lynton drew his cousin's arm into his own and escorted her towards Miss Mallet.

"Lynton," hissed Thalia desperately as they neared her governess. "When will you bring me into the company of the pretty horsebreakers?"

"I will inform Letty of my plans," Lynton hissed back, speaking out of the corner of his mouth and keeping his teeth clenched in a great smile. "She will be able to tell you when you call upon her tomorrow."

"It must be soon, Lynton," Thalia warned as they approached Miss Mallet. Lynton muttered back, "It will be, I assure you," followed immediately by a cordial greeting to the excited governess, who was still shrieking Thalia's name.

"Miss Mallet, how glad I am that you have been able to find us," Lynton said charmingly. "Thalia had been most distraught. We have been searching for you everywhere but when we could not locate you I thought it best for us to remain quietly in the shade so as not to call attention to Thalia's lack of a chaperone."

Miss Mallet was not immediately mollified by this. When she had approached the two, Thalia, except for the plainness of her costume, could easily have been mistaken for one of the unfortunate fallen women who procured young men in the Park.

"I thank you for your thoughtfulness, Mr. Lanston," she said formally, and with some suspicion in her voice, for she knew that Mrs. Horrocks considered Lynton a thoroughly disreputable young man. "Thalia, mount your horse immediately, please, and let us leave as quickly as possible." Their departure, however, was as slow as their arrival, for the Park was still thronged with people. Both rode in silence for quite some time, for Thalia was occupied in planning a stunning costume for her forthcoming Adventure, and Miss Mallet was trying to decide what course to take when Mrs. Horrocks asked about her daughter's conduct in the Park.

In the end, she thought it best to say nothing, for Mrs. Horrocks would certainly take her to task for allowing Thalia to evade her surveillance and it would be difficult to explain exactly how this had occurred. Ever since she had been hired by Mrs. Horrocks, ten years ago, after the abrupt death of Thalia's father, she had found the girl unmanageable. It was not that Thalia was a wicked child; Miss Mallet had had her share of wicked children — that horrid Wainwright boy for one. She still shuddered at the thought of him. Thalia, on the contrary, had simply been unable to understand why the behaviour that was most natural to her was considered unacceptable by others, and Miss Mallet realized with despair that all of her gentle speeches had no effect whatsoever. She could not bring herself to be cruel or overly stern for she knew that the injudicious use of authority had an exactly contrary effect upon Thalia, who would immediately turn around and do what was forbidden, merely for the sake of exerting what little freedom of action she had.

Yet as Thalia grew older, Miss Mallet found it increasingly difficult to supervise her at every moment of the day, and she herself thought it very likely that Mrs. Horrocks would soon realize that she required a younger and more authoritarian governess for her eldest daughter and would dismiss the long-suffering Miss Mallet. It was for this reason that Miss Mallet decided to remain silent; she could not take another position at her age, and she was deeply devoted to the wayward Thalia, and to the less likeable but perfectly docile Flora. However, her decision to protect Thalia and herself from the rage of Mrs. Horrocks did not excuse Thalia's disgraceful conduct. Taking advantage of their slow progress down Oxford Street, Miss Mallet began to deliver another of her standard lectures, much to the amusement of those in nearby carriages.

Chapter Two

*In Which Thalia Sets Her Scheme into Action
and Effects a Bold Escape*

DINNER WAS, AS USUAL, a very depressing affair. The dining parlour was a sombre room, panelled in oak; the windows were shrouded with heavy red velvet draperies edged in gilt. The only light radiated from the candles in the huge, ornate silver candlesticks at either end of the table. Their fitful light flashed on the cut crystal glasses, creating dancing rainbow patterns on the white damask cloth. To one side, looming up ominously out of the darkness, was the enormous mahogany sideboard with its pink variegated marble top. The butler, the silent Mr. Carter, stood beside it, ready to hand down the side dishes.

Mr. Horrocks sat at the head of the table, beneath his portrait on the wall. The portrait showed a stern, heavy-set man with a shock of abundant black hair, a large dark moustache, and thick bushy eyebrows. The portrait painter had not been an artist; he had merely brushed upon the canvas the surface resemblance of a man, with no animation of humour in his features. However, the man below the portrait appeared little more alive than the picture itself: only the ruddiness of his cheeks and the unusually lowering line of his brows distinguished him from it and betrayed that he was motivated by the human passions, in this case, anger. Money had slowly been disappearing at the bank of which he was the junior partner and today the investigation had penetrated into the confines of his own office. The senior partner had dared to suggest that he had been guilty of negligence; he looked around the table grimly, ready to wreak vengeance upon any member of his family who would give him cause.

He looked towards his wife, noting with approval that she was dressed in the appropriate manner for a woman of her position. She wore, as usual, her purple mousseline evening gown with small gold earrings at her ears and a huge gold and ruby necklace clasped about her throat. Her thick chestnut brown hair was pinned back into its customary chignon, making her plump face appear more than necessarily severe.

She gazed back at her husband placidly. The dinner hour was one of her favourite times of the day, as it affirmed her belief in the solidity of her marriage and home. She felt great pride, seeing the elaborately patterned Worcester dinner service, the ruby-coloured Venetian goblets in the glass cupboard. For a long time now she had felt the deep security of knowing that her life was flowing smoothly in the proper channels, yet, remembering the past, she cherished this domestic tranquillity as her most valuable possession.

She had been married when only sixteen to the charming but penniless younger brother of the present Viscount Lanston. As the only child of a fabulously wealthy City merchant, she had brought an immense fortune to Lawrence Lanston, and had hoped in turn that the marriage would confer upon her an entree to the elite circles of the upper classes, the dream her papa had always cherished for his plain but rich daughter. The nightmare had begun at her wedding from which the Lanstons had been conspicuously and completely absent. Scorned by her in-laws, the new Mrs. Lanston had repudiated all association with the aristocracy and determined to live instead upon her money and her infatuation for her handsome if unfaithful husband. It was shocking that only eight years later, when he was shot to death by an irate husband who found Lawrence in bed with his wife, she had felt little pity or sorrow. She had long since ceased to love him; he was categorized in her mind as a further example of that malicious type, the aristocrat, who sapped upon the strength of those like herself and her father who had struggled through years of poverty and suffering to acquire a respectable position in the world.

Through his gratification of one weak and foolish passion, typical of the many affairs which he had conducted while she bore his name, he had destroyed the facade of gentility which she had finally acquired. It was, in fact, fortunate that he had died when he did, for within another year he could also have brought her again to the depths of the poverty from which her father had raised her so carefully; his costly presents of emerald bracelets and matched pairs to his lights of love had almost depleted her vast inheritance.

Determined not to expose herself again to such shame, the widow had waited the appropriate two years of mourning and then quietly married Mr. Harold Horrocks, her late husband's banker, who had provided invaluable aid throughout the humiliating days of paying off debts owed to jewellers and carriage-makers, and even to some of the most notorious gaming hells and brothels in London. They had quickly set up a new household in the very unfashionable, yet very respectable, Russell Square, and the new Mrs. Horrocks set about inexorably eliminating every trace of her previous marriage. Their furniture was new, glossy and huge and overly ornate; their household staff was new, with the exception of Mr. Horrocks' valet, who had cared for him in his bachelor chambers; even their friends were new, rich merchants and barristers and bankers, like her father and her husband, who had all the wealth and power of the aristocracy without the appendage of a useless title.

Unfortunately Mrs. Horrocks could not obliterate all traces of her past, for she had acquired two daughters by Lawrence Lanston. The younger, Flora, now thirteen years of age, was dear to her mother, of whom she was a miniature replica, having inherited her mother's tendency to plumpness, her drab-coloured hair, and her expressionless brown eyes. Thalia, however, was a sore affront, for she had many of the features of her father. She was a thin, vibrant girl with masses of dark, curly hair which would not stay back no matter how severely pinned but strayed about her neck in loose tendrils. She also had her father's bold and handsome dark eyes and his delicate, aristocratic bone structure. But her mother feared most that she had inherited his weakness of character and was always on the watch for the slightest proof of this suspicion. Lawrence had idolized his daughter and taken her with him on all occasions without the slightest discretion. Mrs. Horrocks believed that the young girl had been introduced into the depths of fast society and been witness to many scenes of depravity and dissolution. After Flora's birth, Lawrence, who was a great admirer of female beauty, had ignored his younger daughter completely, realizing that she had inherited her mother's dowdiness. He left her instead to the ministrations of her mother, who poured out all of her frustrated affection upon this plain girl.

It had, in all events, not turned out for the best. Even the doting Mrs. Horrocks was forced to admit that Flora was spoilt and shallow, while Thalia, who had withdrawn entirely for many years after her father's death, and who still refused to call Mr. Horrocks "Papa," was becoming more assertive and impertinent.

Mrs. Horrocks now had three children by Mr. Horrocks and she anticipated the day when she could marry off her two elder daughters and devote herself entirely to the arduous task of bringing up the younger Horrockses in the proper manner.

Meanwhile, however, the children were in the nursery under the watchful eye of the young nursemaid and, having noticed her husband's ill humour, it was her duty, as the guardian of domestic harmony, to assure that the two girls behaved creditably. At the moment they were dressed in their matching cherry-pink-and-buff-striped evening dresses. Flora unfortunately did not look her best in pink. It brought out the sallowness of her complexion and took the lustre from her hair. Thalia, on the other hand, glowed, but Mrs. Horrocks noted with disapproval that the bodice of the dress was too tight and the décolletage too low. She reminded herself to speak to her dressmaker about designing two new matching outfits, for Thalia's dress would have to be discarded; she had grown out of it. Her table manners, however, appeared impeccable, while Flora was gobbling her soup like a little pig.

Unfortunately Thalia soon destroyed this momentary illusion of good behaviour by giggling.

She had glanced up to see Miss Mallet, who was sitting in semi-darkness at one comer of the large table. Mrs. Horrocks considered it a waste of time and effort to have a separate meal prepared and brought up to the governess in her tiny third-floor bedroom; therefore, she was permitted to dine with the family when there were no guests. Miss Mallet was more intimidated than was usual; she still could not believe that she had replied "Admirably" to Mrs. Horrocks' inquiry about how Thalia had conducted herself at the Park. She was certain that her lie would be momentarily discovered; unable to look at the others at the table, she stared instead into her soup, sipping it off her spoon with delicate slurps. Thalia, noticing her small, timid eyes and her quivering nose (always a sign of distress in Miss Mallet) suddenly visualized her governess as a huge, overgrown rabbit.

Striving to repress the fit of the giggles which was the result of this vision, she bent over her own soup bowl, thereby missing the angry glare which her mother turned upon her. Fortunately Mr. Horrocks had remarked nothing. As he had finished his first course, he signalled for Carter to remove the plates, which was done so quickly that Miss Mallet was left with a spoonful of soup halfway to her mouth.

In the pause while the entree was being placed upon the table, Mr. Horrocks turned to his elder stepdaughter.

"How will you spend your day tomorrow, Miss Thalia?" he asked gruffly.

"I plan to visit Letty," Thalia replied, looking up quickly.

"Letitia," corrected Mrs. Horrocks. She abhorred the use of sobriquets, which she considered familiar and offensive. She was grateful that although Thalia's true father had insisted on calling the girl by the fanciful name of Thalia, at least it was a name which could not be shortened. "You visited Letitia only this morning, Thalia. It would be an imposition upon the Lanstons' hospitality if you were to call upon her again tomorrow."

"She was in the process of teaching me an embroidery stitch which I need to finish off properly the edges of the leaves on the seat cover I am doing, Mama," Thalia lied dutifully. "It is very difficult and I am not yet able to do it myself."

"That's not true, Mama," shrieked Flora from her side of the table, but she was quickly silenced by Mr. Horrocks.

"Flora, you were not spoken to. If you interrupt the conversation once more in that manner, you will be sent from the table," he said, the pent-up wrath of the day descending upon the unwitting Flora like an avalanche. She lapsed into a sulky silence, sending venomous looks at Thalia from across the table. Miss Mallet, who also had reason to believe that Thalia was telling an untruth, blinked her eyes rapidly and tried to shrink back farther into the shadows.

"Mrs. Horrocks," said Mr. Horrocks, "I thought you had instilled better manners into your daughters. Flora should certainly have learned by now that one thing which I will not tolerate is being interrupted. And," he continued, directing his remarks to his wife, "I do not understand why you object to Thalia calling upon her cousin. You have often told me that Letitia Lanston is a very sweet and obedient girl and that you hoped association with her would have a beneficial effect upon the formation of *your* daughter's character." Feeling that in some way his wife and Flora were responsible for his discomfort, he turned indulgently to Thalia and remarked, "I am sure that for such a good purpose, you may be permitted to visit your cousin tomorrow," and then turned his attention to the roast, the haunch of mutton, and the capons being placed upon the table.

Thus, in the morning, when Thalia appeared dressed in her calling costume at Mrs. Horrocks' sitting-room door, her mother could make no objection. She merely remarked bitingly that Thalia looked quite untidy and that she expected her return within an hour, as it surely could not take much longer to learn one embroidery stitch. Feeling that Divine Providence surely favoured the writing of her Novel, Thalia learned with even greater surprise that Miss Mallet would be unable to accompany her, as the governess's experience was required in the nursery where the young and yet untrained nursemaid was having great problems controlling the three younger Horrockses. She was to be chaperoned only by

Joseph, the coachman, who would wait for her outside the Lanston house; she realized gratefully that she would be able to speak to Letty in strictest confidence.

However, one factor which she had not anticipated was that Letty herself would be opposed to Thalia's plans. When she was ushered into Letty's private sitting room, her cousin fell upon her, exclaiming,

"Thalia, Lynton told me all last night. It is too horrifying. You cannot mean to go through with it."

Thalia seated herself upon a small, delicate chair and stared at Letty aghast.

"What has Lynton told you?" she asked.

Letty was pacing up and down the carpet before the mantel, driven by her concern for her cousin.

"Thalia, it is most shocking!" she replied, looking at her beseechingly. "Lynton has told me that you have asked him to take you into the company of—no—I cannot say it— into the company of—of—disreputable females. Thalia, you cannot know how degraded these women are. Well, I own I cannot know myself, never having met one, but Thalia, think what effect they could have upon you. If you were seen in their company, if you picked up quite innocently one of their mannerisms, why any gentleman would know immediately and think less honourably of you. It distresses me greatly, Thalia, dear cousin," she sat down opposite Thalia and took her hands into her own, "but I cannot aid you in this. I implore you not to ask it of me."

"But has Lynton told you of my reasons?" asked Thalia, and, seeing the blank look in Letty's eyes, continued, "No, I am sure he did not. He would not think it important."

She proceeded to relate to Letty the sad story which she had told to Lynton, stressing heavily the impending marriage to the odious Frederic Cornfield. Letty, having reasons of her own to feel sympathy for someone being forced into a loveless match, was cast into great doubt. "Thalia, is there no other way? Is there no other type of novel which would suit?" she inquired. But having been reassured by her impetuous cousin that there were no alternatives, she sighed and said firmly, "If I am to help you in this, you must make me several promises."

Eagerly Thalia agreed to dress modestly, to use a false name (together they decided she should be Thalia Lawrence, taking her father's personal name for her pseudonym) and to speak only to one or two of the most respectable "females," as Letty called them. Having exacted these promises from Thalia with a stern countenance, Letty agreed to allow her to borrow a dress, as this would permit her to have some supervision over Thalia's choice, and they slipped up to Letty's bedroom to choose the garment.

Thalia was thrown into raptures by the costumes in Letty's wardrobe. She danced across the room, holding first one and then another before her and smiling at herself in the mirror. As Letty was often required to attend three or four of the most exclusive parties in one evening, and as her father expected her to catch a rich marquis or earl for a husband, she owned many exquisite evening and ball dresses. And it was to these charming creations that Thalia was immediately attracted, dresses of the thinnest, lightest silk with huge skirts, looped and gathered with tiny flowers or ruffled and tied with flimsy bows. But Letitia, planning to make Thalia as inconspicuous as possible, had different ideas. She held out one after the other her plainest costumes, all impeccably designed and carried out, but in dark, unobtrusive colours and with a minimum of frills. In the end they compromised. Thalia gave in meekly and accepted a plain cream-coloured dress with yards of flounces around the skirts and rich lace draping the sleeves and neckline. Letitia noted with satisfaction that Thalia looked like a young and innocent young girl in this simple dress, but Thalia observed that the absence of colour made her dark curls and dark eyes even more striking and brought a rosy pink to her cheeks. She flaunted herself before the mirror, fluttering her lashes and sweeping the flounces about in a spiral of curtseys, until Letty prevailed upon her to take it off and put on again the plain, dark blue outfit in which she had arrived. It was long past the hour which Thalia had been allotted by her mother, and it was not until they were hurrying through the great marble passage towards the front door, with the dress concealed beneath Thalia's cloak, that Thalia realized she had not yet discovered how or when she was to meet Lynton.

"Letty," she exclaimed, halting abruptly and causing her cousin to crash into her, "where is Lynton planning to take me?"

Letty looked pale and whispered nervously, "To Cremorne. I begged him not to take you there, for as you know no respectable woman has gone there for many years now, but he said it would easier for you to pass unnoticed and to only speak to those— females—who seemed most respectable. He wishes that you will meet him at eight o'clock in Russell Square before your house. He will be waiting in a hired coach and take you up immediately." She looked around quickly to be sure that no servants who could have heard this shocking proposal were nearby.

Thalia's eyes widened. "Oh Letty! Cremorne! How very exciting!" she exclaimed. "I promise I shall tell you all that happens." Letty, who would not for the world have admitted that she was interested in this subject, was secretly pleased that her courageous cousin would bring so much adventure into her own sheltered life.

"You must take care, Thalia," she admonished her. "You must remember all you have promised."

"I shall," said Thalia, smiling, "and Letty, I am truly grateful that you are my cousin." She hugged her as well as she could, hampered by the circumference of her own and Letty's crinolines, and then dashed down the front steps and into the waiting carriage.

The remainder of her day passed uneventfully. Thalia was forced to invent a new embroidery stitch to demonstrate to her mama and, in doing so, tangled her thread so much that the seat cover was almost destroyed while she was cutting out the knotted strands. Mrs. Horrocks despaired of her daughter's ever becoming a proficient needlewoman.

After the solemn family dinner and the nightly Bible reading, the ladies adjourned as usual to the drawing room. As Mr. Horrocks had closeted himself in his study, the two girls were not required to play the piano and sing for his evening entertainment. Instead, they read quietly and continued sewing by the flickering light of the gas lamps. Thalia, however, upon this occasion, excused herself after a short time, saying that she was unusually fatigued and left the room with a graceful curtsey and a dutiful kiss for her mother. Mrs. Horrocks began to think that her rebellious daughter might yet acquire the good manners of a lady and put it down to Letitia's good influence, deciding that she would permit Thalia to call upon her cousin more often.

Meanwhile Thalia was dressing herself by the light of a candle in her borrowed finery. It was difficult to fasten the row of tiny buttons down the back of the dress but she managed somehow. Letty had imagined that Thalia would be quite unremarkable in the simple, plain-coloured dress, but she had not taken into account Thalia's nature.

Thalia had promised to be of credit to her cousin Lynton and so she was determined to be. Ascertaining his taste in female dress from the outrageous attire of the young lady in the blue phaeton in the Park, she took down her serviceable dark blue serge cloak. Mrs. Horrocks had considered this quite suitable for her daughters, as practicality was of more importance than frivolity, but fortunately the cloak had a bright red satin lining, and when it was turned inside out, the dark blue appeared to be merely a border.

The problem of a fashionable hat was solved with a little more ingenuity. Mrs. Horrocks had recently seen fit to give her daughters the pork-pie hats which were all the mode; the fact that the plume atop this hat was innocently white had not deterred Thalia in the least. With a set of paints borrowed from the schoolroom she had spent the better part of an hour elaborately dyeing it to a glorious red. With the feather inserted back into the ribbon around the hat brim, and the red cloak about her dress, Thalia, observing herself in the mirror, admitted that she looked most striking.

The only remaining problem was how to exit from the house unobtrusively. There was little likelihood that Mrs. Horrocks would discover her daughter's absence for the bedroom door locked from within and Mrs. Horrocks had long discontinued the practice of coming in to kiss her daughters goodnight as she considered this a dubious and unnecessary display of a little-felt affection. As Mr. Horrocks was firmly settled into the study and her mother and younger sister were doubtlessly still occupied in the drawing room, Thalia could not leave through the front entrance. But there was a door from the kitchen which led into the stable yard and it was not likely that anyone would be there, as the dishes from dinner had long been washed and put away.

Tiptoeing silently down the grand carpeted staircase Thalia entered the kitchen and found it, as she had expected, deserted. She passed noiselessly through the silent ghostly room, past the huge range and enormous planked table, and slipped out the side door. Then, after running quickly alongside the curtained windows, she was out into the street and across to the quiet seclusion of the empty square.

It was a foggy night; the tawdry yellow London fog was swirling about the lamp posts, and from her vantage point across the street Thalia could barely discern the outline of her home. She was not frightened at being alone in the foggy night, for she enjoyed the sense of mystery and adventure which it conveyed. She had often gazed out of her bedroom window, imagining a handsome dark stranger who would appear below mounted on a huge black horse. In her dreams she would somehow contrive to exit through the too small window and fall into his arms. Together they would ride off to a magical sunny countryside, while London would melt away from them on either side in the fog.

Chapter Three

In Which Thalia Goes to Cremorne Gardens and St. Johns Wood and Meets Many of the Notorious Inhabitants of the London Demimonde

LYNTON, ALTHOUGH BLOND-HAIRED and blue-eyed, appeared in a suitably mysterious manner, materializing in one moment beneath a street lamp and pulling her up beside him to the seat in the hackney coach. In a moment they were off, the tired horses plodding solemnly through the foggy streets. Thalia's heart pounded rapidly with excitement and she gazed out of the dusty windows, suddenly aware of the incredible variety of people in the streets.

Lynton while they drove was in deep thought. His sister Letitia had been hounding him all evening about the impropriety of taking his innocent cousin to Cremorne Gardens. He had often gone there with friends and knew that usually only the lower classes of prostitutes frequented the Gardens, yet he could hardly bring Thalia into one of the casinos or dancing rooms where she would have been immediately noticed and commented upon. He hoped that at Cremorne he would be able to keep her in seclusion down one of the less frequented paths until he ascertained whether there were any light-skirts present whom he could discreetly introduce to her. He had reviewed all those of his acquaintance but most of them had been passing fancies and he no longer knew how to find them.

His most recent "friends" had been those of the Skittles type, crude, vulgar girls who made no secret of their low upbringings, a refreshing change from the simpering misses he was partnered with at parties, but not at all the type of girl for Thalia to meet. In fact, he suspected that most of them would be quite cruel to her as they often were to those of their own kind, their charm being reserved instead for the gentlemen.

By the time they had reached the entrance to Cremorne, Lynton was quite downcast. This adventure, which had seemed so simple in the sunny afternoon, now seemed a difficult duty and he was dubious about its outcome. His scheme to keep Thalia in the background was destroyed by Thalia herself, who was charmed by Cremorne and insisted on running about the many paths and walks and exclaiming excitedly about the pavilions and the dancing.

However, after her initial enthusiasm at being outdoors in a seeming fairyland of flowerbeds and groves with multi-coloured lanterns twinkling overhead in the fog, Thalia began to feel quite uncomfortable. There were quite a number of gentlemen present, all rather seedy-looking, and they gave Thalia bold, impertinent stares as Lynton hurried her past them. The females were also intimidating. Heavily rouged, in elaborate dresses of bright colours, they paraded about, flaunting themselves before the men and ogling them with suggestive glances. Their voices were shrill, they laughed loudly and raucously, and the language they used made Thalia ill at ease although she could not understand the greater part of it.

She was grateful when Lynton steered her into a leafy bower from which she could watch the dancers unobserved, while he strode out onto the path to look around for a suitable female. He considered that if he could find just one, she and Thalia could have a brief talk and then he could hurry his cousin out of this disreputable place and back to her respectable home, his duty having been discharged. If this was done soon enough he could return to Cremorne or one of the more fashionable night places and procure for himself some feminine company as a reward for having successfully accomplished his difficult task. At the present, however, he despaired of a solution and in order to help settle his troubled thoughts he groped in his pocket for a cigar.

At this moment, he felt a female hand upon his arm and a voice behind him asking amusedly, "Are you good-natured, sir?"

Turning about, he saw a lovely young girl of about Thalia's age with thick, tawny hair, large golden eyes, and small, lovely pink lips. Her slender body, encased in an expensive gown of palest orange, was full and voluptuous; Lynton felt a throb of desire, but the problem of his cousin was more immediately pressing.

"Can you repeat what you just said?" he demanded quickly.

The girl smiled slowly; her golden eyes danced with amusement.

"You may not have heard my words, sir," she said finally, "but you certainly understood my meaning." She looked at him steadfastly with the same amused smile, her hands placed provocatively upon her hips.

But Lynton had heard what he wished. Her voice was clear and musical; she spoke with the cultured intonation of someone of the upper classes. And he noted with approval that she had little powder upon her face and that her costume was of impeccable good taste.

"Do you swear?" he asked with great eagerness and haste in his voice.

Upon this remark, the girl smiled again. She had an irresistible smile, beginning slowly as if she was trying to suppress her mirth and gradually widening until even her eyes were smiling.

"How very provocative," she said at last. "What an unusual approach."

"But do you swear?" Lynton asked again impatiently. The girl gave him a sideways glance, as if she feared he had been recently let loose from Bedlam.

However seeing the concerned look in his eyes, she replied slowly, "No I do not. It is not to my taste. I know that it is fashionable just now but it is not the manner in which I choose to present myself."

"Then you are just the girl I have been looking for," Lynton said, clasping her by the hand and dragging her abruptly towards the bench where Thalia sat. He noticed with approval that her hand was cool and smooth beneath his fingers and that she held his hand with a firm and confident grasp. But his greatest concern at the moment was to introduce her to Thalia before she disappeared back into the fog from which she had come; the urgings of his body could be ignored until later in the evening.

As soon as they were within a few steps of Thalia, who looked up with startled eyes, Lynton paused and, turning to his newfound prize, inquired her name in a low voice. Then he turned proudly to his cousin, and in the manner of a proprietor showing his wares, proclaimed, "Miss Thalia Lawrence, I would like to present to you Miss Susannah Stillwater." The introduction having been accomplished, he added importantly, "She does not swear, you know." Susannah looked at him again in amazement, and Thalia, realizing the absurdity of the situation, began to giggle.

"Thank you, dearest cousin," she said. "Will you go and procure some refreshments for Miss Stillwater and myself, and I will explain this entire situation to her." Seeing his reluctance, she added, "I am quite safe here, Lynton. Miss Stillwater shall protect me. Please have a seat."

"Susannah," murmured Miss Stillwater as she settled down upon the bench next to Thalia, "please do explain. I am most confused."

"Then you must call me Thalia," replied that young lady as Lynton went off to do her bidding. "It is really absurdly simple. You see I intend to write a Novel about the pretty horsebreakers and I begged my cousin Lynton to bring me here so that he could introduce me to one. But he has been most distressed all evening because he was determined that I should only speak with respectable females. And now he has found you he feels quite proud."

Susannah could not suppress another smile. This was really the most ridiculous pair of persons she had ever met at Cremorne, where there were many odd people indeed. She would have thought that this young girl was also one of the muslin company because of her gaudy red cloak, but for her earnest brown eyes and innocent air. Upon closer inspection, she realized the cloak was a plain serge one turned wrong side out, and she noticed another peculiarity.

"What are those odd streaks upon your hat, my dear?" she inquired politely.

"Oh dear!" exclaimed Thalia, pulling off the offending article and staring at it glumly. "The paint has come off." She turned to Susannah. "You see, I did not have anything quite flashy enough to wear in Lynton's company so I used some paint and dyed the feather red. But now it has spoiled the entire hat, and it was a new one. I do not know what Mama will do to me or how I can possibly explain this to her."

"You must have the entire hat dyed red so the stains will not show," Susannah suggested.

"But I cannot," Thalia cried despairingly, "I am never let out of the house unaccompanied, and I have no ready money of my own. Just a pittance of an allowance which my stepfather gives us to buy ribbons and gloves." She stared sadly at the unfortunate hat in her hands.

Susannah was made quite uncomfortable by Thalia's rapid down-slide from high good spirits into the deepest fit of melancholy.

"I could take the hat and have it dyed by my milliner," she offered, not knowing quite why she did so. A further thought came to her mind, one which would be of some benefit to herself. "Then your cousin could call upon me and retrieve it for you," she added, for she was anxious to see more of the handsome young man who had departed in search of refreshments. "Yes, I am sure that is what we must do," she concluded.

Thalia's eyes began to glow again; neither she nor Susannah had thought of the difficulty entailed in explaining to Mrs. Horrocks why a once white hat had become red overnight. "You are very gracious," she said, smiling her most engaging smile.

Susannah again felt uncomfortable. What was she doing in the company of this absurdly charming but innocent young girl and her seemingly mad cousin? Yet, she reminded herself, she had come to Cremorne only in search of amusement and these two were certainly providing her with that.

"Tell me about your novel," she demanded, interested in knowing what a well-bred young miss knew of the pretty horse-breakers.

"I have not yet thought of a Plot," Thalia confessed. "I only thought that if the Heroine were a pretty horsebreaker then many people would buy it. I suppose I will explain about her childhood, and how she becomes one of the pretty horsebreakers, and then at the end she will marry a duke or a marquis? Does that sound suitable?"

"It is rather a meagre plot," Susannah replied. "You shall have to create a very fascinating heroine if you wish your audience to read to the end."

"May I use you for a Heroine?" Thalia inquired shyly. Susannah smiled her slow, amused grin once more. "I regret that my life has been rather uninteresting. I am sure I would not do as a heroine."

Thalia was downcast again. "I must write this Novel," she said sadly. "You see it is the only way that I can escape from the domination of my mother, who is a dragon, and my odious stepfather, and my equally odious sister Flora. I am determined to be independent but I did not know how to accomplish it until I chanced upon the idea of writing a Novel."

"Why, you must marry," Susannah said, suggesting the only proper escape for a young girl of Thalia's class. "Then you will have your own establishment and be able to live exactly as you like."

"No," retorted Thalia stubbornly, "I will not marry. I have seen enough of marriage to know that it would be an escape into another kind of bondage. I have no wish to bring up passels of little whining children and supervise the running of a household. And my mama is planning that I marry Frederic Cornfield, the son of one of my stepfather's business friends. I am sure she would not permit me to marry anyone amusing, and marriage to Frederic Cornfield would be a living death."

Susannah, who had not meant at all to be drawn into this tangled web of problems, found herself feeling an instant camaraderie for Thalia. She reminded Susannah of herself, when at a tender age she had determined to free herself from the bondage of household service, acquire a house of her own and a life which she could determine, without the impediment of a demanding husband. Thalia's views on marriage and independence were the same as her own; her vitality and courage were remarkable assets in such a young and protected girl.

"I will help you," she said earnestly, regretting her words even as she said them. "I see now that you must write a novel and if I can aid you in any way I will be most pleased to do so."

Thalia did not find this at all out of the ordinary. She had quite forgotten that Susannah was one of the notorious pretty horse-breakers and was treating her as a confidante in the same manner as she treated Letty.

"Then, if you cannot be my Heroine," Thalia said instantly, "you must introduce me to someone who will do. I am sure you know such a person."

Susannah was surprised by this show of confidence; she began to think that Thalia would be able to accomplish what few women did and, by writing her novel, free herself from the domestic tyranny under which so many young misses suffered. As soon as she had applied herself to the problem of a fascinating heroine she knew instantly the solution.

"Lady Guenevere," she exclaimed abruptly. "I am certain that she is your heroine. She is a very good friend of mine, a beautiful woman, refined and intelligent, but a bit eccentric. You see she lives out her fancies rather than merely dreaming them. Last year she wished to be an Italian Contessa, whereupon she instantly changed her name, the decor of her home, and even her lovers. This year, having taken a liking to Tennyson, she has decided to live in the Gothic Ages and therefore calls herself Lady Guenevere. You could meet her tonight if you wished; there is always a small gathering of friends at her villa in St. John's Wood. And they are the most cultured people; the gentlemen come as much to talk with her and admire her beautiful collection of art objects as to acclaim her beauty. As soon as your cousin returns we must ask him to take us there."

"How exciting!" exclaimed Thalia, but before the words were barely past her lips a strong male arm, clothed in a black jacket, reached through the opening of the bushes behind them and fumbled at the neckline of Thalia's dress. Thalia gasped, and clutching the hand firmly thrust it from her, taking the opportunity to bite it strongly before she pushed it aside. There was an exclamation of pain and several muttered oaths from beyond the bushes and then a gentleman's face appeared. He was handsome in a rugged way, with heavy dark eyebrows and black hair; a wry smile twisted his thick moustache upwards, giving him quite a forbidding appearance.

"Susannah," he said in a voice slurred with drink. "You must teach your pretty companion better manners if she is to be a success. Damn the girl! What can she be about attacking me in this manner?"

"Jack," Susannah said harshly, rising up from her seat, and pulling Thalia behind her. She glared at him angrily, "She is not what you think. Leave your bloody hands off." She paused, her eyes flashing, her cheeks flushed with anger, quite unaware that she had broken her resolution not to swear. Thalia was beginning to tremble, partly from the fright of the previous moment, and partly from the cold night air. Susannah, sensing this, put one arm about her protectively.

The man she referred to as Jack seemed amused by this. His body was still concealed behind the bushes so that only his face, snarling out of the fog appeared as some kind of demon apparition. "A touching picture, my lovelies," he sneered, with an amused lift of his eyebrows. "I swear you could stand for a portrait by one of our sentimental artists, entitled 'Angel of the Gutter and a Poor Waif.' Not to mind, I will not disturb the composition, but—" he tipped his hat in Thalia's direction "—do not think that I shall forget you, my little darling."

"That Beast!" spat out Susannah, as he disappeared back into the fog. "The Baron Croydon, the latest in a long line of cads and bounders. Regretfully they have all been extremely wealthy and can easily satisfy their basest appetites. In all of London you could not find a truer Villain. What can your cousin have been thinking, bringing you to Cremorne? And where is he now? We must leave immediately!"

This roused Thalia from her temporary passivity and she managed to swear Susannah to silence about the incident, asserting that she was more surprised than afraid and that she did not wish her future plans to be disrupted by these events.

Lynton appeared shortly, trying clumsily to balance a tray holding three once full, now half-empty, glasses. It had taken him quite a while, for he had spent some time in the company of various lovely girls who importuned him, having to refill his glass of sherry frequently as it became empty. He now brought with him his third glass as well as two lemonades for the ladies. He had wondered if Susannah would prefer something stronger, but as he was forced to offer lemonade to his cousin, he had decided that he should bring the other lady the same. However, Susannah accepted her lemonade with good humour and thanked Lynton prettily with a dazzling glance from her amber eyes.

Lynton had many fleeting reservations about his cousin's continued presence at Cremorne. He also doubted his wisdom in leaving her alone for so long with a lady of easy virtue. Therefore, as soon as she had quaffed the last of her lemonade he suggested that he should return her immediately to her home.

He was much taken aback when she became indignant. "Oh no, Lynton!" she protested. "Susannah has just promised to take us to the home of her friend who will be the Heroine for my Novel."

"Lady Guenevere Shalott," Susannah murmured. "Do you know of her?"

Lynton indeed had heard of the eccentric courtesan and the exclusive gatherings at her home in St. John's Wood, but no one of his friends had ever been there. The company was of the highest order; invitations did not extend much below the ranks of marquises among the nobility, although Lady Guenevere was known to take a liking to the strangest persons, flower girls and coachmen, and bring them into the midst of her fashionable guests. Already Lynton pictured himself relating this adventure proudly to his friends at the club the next day.

Therefore, he accepted the proposal and all three set off in search of a hansom cab. As they left the Gardens, Thalia looked about her timidly, fearing that the man named Baron Croydon was still lurking about, but she could not see him among the groups of swells strolling down the walkways.

The coach which they hired was old and had seen much use; the straw at their feet was wet and smelled unpleasantly of odours better left unnamed. Lynton was crushed into a corner by the width of both ladies' crinolines. The iron in their hems cut into his legs and he would have preferred to ride above with the coachman but for the presence of Susannah. He tried to peruse her features and figure unobtrusively, but the interior of the cab was very dim, and whenever they passed beneath a streetlamp, her eyes were always fixed on his with the golden, speculative stare of a self-satisfied cat. He found himself wondering if he could spend the night with her and vowing to find some way to bring this to pass.

When the coach presently came to a stop before a large house blazing with lights, Lynton jumped down first and aided the ladies as they exited, taking this opportunity to place his arm about Susannah's waist and thereby discovering that she had a very warm and compliant body.

From without the house appeared much the same as its neighbours. It was built of light-coloured Portland stone with a row of ornate windows on the ground floor and an imposing doorway. But as they entered the hallway, Susannah introducing herself to the jovial butler and claiming the others as her friends, Thalia felt herself transported to the Gothic Ages. The passage was paved with stone and the walls panelled in a dark wood. The only light blazed from the flaming torches set upon the walls. These quivered back and forth from the draught caused by the opening door and shone upon the strangest assortment of objects Thalia had ever seen. A huge gleaming suit of armour stood in one comer, clutching a lance and looking as if he was about to lunge upon the visitors. Silk pennants in bright colours with bold designs fluttered from the high ceiling. Stone gargoyles with evil, laughing faces peeped out from the shadows. Upon one wall, in a small wooden cage, was what appeared to be a large stuffed owl, but as they passed beneath him, he opened his baleful orange eyes and uttered a disdainful hoot.

The butler with a bouncy step and a shining ruddy face had preceded them down this ghostly passage and was now throwing open a large door and calling out Susannah's name. Conversation within the drawing room ceased for a moment and the guests turned to scrutinize the newcomers while Thalia stopped abruptly at the threshold. She did not even notice the clusters of elegantly dressed ladies and gentlemen present. Her attention was drawn immediately to the far end of the room where a beautiful woman with her thick, curly, dark hair let loose down her back and clothed in a medieval gown of golden velvet was posing at an embroidery frame while a portrait painter peered first at her and then at his canvas. His back was to the doorway and he had not noticed the intrusion, but the lady turned her head gracefully from her work and fixed Thalia with her large, dark eyes. Then she espied Susannah behind her and, excusing herself to the painter, who made a little gesture of despair, she rose and moved graciously towards the newcomers. She seemed to float, her velvet gown trailing silently along the carpeted floor, her slender white hands held out in a dramatic gesture of welcome.

"My darling Susannah," she called out in a low, vibrating voice as she neared them. "It is most gracious of you to honour us with your presence."

Susannah made a low curtsey and then, rising slowly, said, "Lady Guenevere, may I present—"

"Mr. Lynton Lanston," interrupted Lynton, coming forward and bowing to kiss the lady's elegant hand.

"And Miss Thalia—" Susannah began.

Thalia, suddenly remembering her pseudonym, interrupted her: "Lawrence." She followed Susannah's lead and curtsied gracefully.

The majesty of Lady Guenevere was such that each immediately responded as if in the presence of royalty. Lynton had never kissed a woman's hand before, but it had seemed to him the natural thing to do at the moment, and he was now staring at her unabashedly, amazed at her great beauty.

Susannah was unaccountably annoyed by this. She moved forward, saying, "You must not interrupt your sitting, lady, for us. I shall introduce my friends to your other guests."

"But first," the lady said, "you must view the progress of Mr. Rossetti's picture. He has almost completed my portion of it, but alas, he has yet to find a suitable girl to pose as my handmaiden." She led them back across the vast drawing room. Lynton, who had not previously shown any sign of having imbibed three glasses of sherry, stumbled over a small velvet footstool, and when Lady Guenevere glanced at him with a question in her dark eyes, he bowed and said gallantly, "Lady, I am drunk with your beauty."

The lady nodded graciously in acknowledgement of this compliment; Susannah, however, tightened her proprietary hold on Lynton's arm.

Thalia was gazing about the room, still not seeing the guests, but observing the strangeness of the decor. Hundreds of wax tapers were the only illumination; they burned in sconces upon the walls and in graceful silver candelabras upon the tables. The walls, which should have been papered with a bold floral pattern and hung with hundreds of pictures, were covered instead with long, exquisite tapestries of hunting scenes and processions. The furniture was plain and simple, of dark oak, massive pieces which glowed under the light of the candles. Long-stemmed white lilies and exotic passionflowers bloomed in crystal vases, casting a sweet odour into the air. These were the only ornaments; there were no knickknacks or framed miniatures or porcelain statues as Thalia would have expected. The very simplicity of the room was breath taking.

At the far end, a sort of dais had been constructed where Lady Guenevere sat for her portrait before an embroidered tapestry which she herself was completing. The oak chair upon which she had been sitting when they entered stood to the left; to the right was a low bench. At the moment, a little serving-girl with untidy hair and a simple black dress was crouched upon it looking timidly at the painter. The picture itself was only half completed; the tapestry was there in glowing golds and scarlets and greens. Lady Guenevere looked out from the canvas, her dark hair framing her pale face and soulful eyes, her pale hands languidly sorting the coloured threads, but to the right only the figure of a girl was sketched in and the painter was toying with this portion at the moment, impatiently directing the serving-girl to assume a more graceful pose.

"Droop!" he was saying in his intense Italian voice. "Wilt! Look as if you were ineffably bored, as if you were listening to the music of the celestial spheres, as if your soul was far away in some Paradise."

The serving-girl merely looked alarmed at these directions. She shifted to an even more awkward position and gazed at her mistress with pathetic eyes. "It is no good, Lady Guenevere," the painter said, turning to the lady. "She simply will not do. She does not understand at all the mood I am trying to create, the mood which you capture so exquisitely."

"His name is Mr. Rossetti," Susannah was whispering to Thalia. "He paints in a new style, one which he calls Pre-Raphaelite, whatever that may be. It is not much appreciated by the critics, I fear, although Mr. Ruskin—"

But her words to Thalia had attracted the painter's attention.

"Why, here is the girl I have been searching for!" he cried, running forward to grasp Thalia by the hand. "Lady Guenevere, why have you not shown her to me before? She is beautiful, she is perfect, she is the girl in my picture, your handmaiden, your daughter!" He was almost dancing with excitement, his dark eyes darting over Thalia noting every detail of her appearance.

"But of course," he said, "you do not see her as I do. This appalling cloak must go." He plucked the offending article from Thalia's shoulders and thrust it aside. "And the hair! Why will young girls pin back their hair in this hideous manner?" His agile fingers were plucking the pins from Thalia's neatly coiled chignon as he said this, scattering them about her in a shower of silver, until she stood with her curly locks let loose down her back.

"The dress of course is incorrect," the painter continued, turning her about, "but the colour is just what I require. That beautiful shade of old lace, the dim mingling of white and shadows. I will naturally alter the details as I paint, but the style itself is simple enough."

He paused to realize that all of those who stood about Thalia and even the girl herself were staring at him in great confusion. "Ah, you still do not see," he exclaimed. He addressed his remarks to Lady Guenevere. "Why she could be your daughter. Observe. The same slender, graceful neck," he said, raising Thalia's chin, "the same beautiful, heavy-lidded, dark eyes with that aura of mystery within them, the same sensuous lips. She even has your bone structure, those high, elegant cheekbones, the slender, delicate hands," he said, possessing himself of one of these and patting it fondly. "Surely you understand," he stated, whirling about and confronting Lynton and Susannah.

"Yes," Susannah replied hesitantly, "there is a resemblance."

"A resemblance!" repeated Mr. Rossetti mockingly. "It is enough. She is perfect." He motioned at the serving-girl who seemed about to run from her post. "Away with you, girl. We no longer require you." Still holding Thalia's hand, he led her up upon the dais and seated her on the bench, asking her to hold a cluster of scarlet floss-silk in her hands and gaze mournfully towards the chair.

"You are a young girl alone in a castle with your mother," he said, waving his hand towards Lady Guenevere. "Your lover is away on the battlefield with your father and your brothers. You fear they may never return alive.

And while they are gone, all you can do is work upon your tapestry. So you sit sadly upon this bench, drooping with sorrow, your hands almost losing their hold upon the silk threads, seeing not the tapestry before you but the war which is raging far away."

Thalia, who had a good sense of the dramatic, quickly understood what was required of her and entered into the mood which the painter had created. He stepped back to observe her. "Lovely," he exclaimed. "Now do not move. I must sketch your position quickly." He ran back behind his canvas and began drawing with rapid gestures.

Slowly the conversation in the room began again; Thalia could sense that Lynton and Susannah had moved away and were talking with the other guests. Only Lady Guenevere remained before the dais, but when Mr. Rossetti informed her that he would not require her pose at the moment she too turned away to mingle with her callers, and Thalia and Mr. Rossetti were left alone in their silent medieval world.

Thalia however soon tired of this and began to cast furtive glances at the company. As Mr. Rossetti did not correct her, she assumed he was not painting "the mournful look" in her eyes and proceeded to look about more boldly. Unfortunately the first person she observed was the evil Baron Croydon, who was perched upon a velvet footstool, sipping from a glass containing a ruby-coloured liquid, and chatting with a young female in a brightly striped red dress. However, he was very much aware of Thalia's presence and turned his head frequently to fix her with what she could only describe as a leer. His thick lips would part slightly, the edges of his moustache would curl up and his eyes narrowed until they appeared to be glittering dark beads. Thalia felt herself begin to shiver, and at the same time, an immense resentment boiled up within her. She looked about for Susannah or Lynton but could not find them in the crowd. The painter seemed totally unaware of her fear and went on with his rapid sketching, talking to himself under his breath.

As she cast about for some protection, Thalia noticed another gentleman lounging languidly across a brocade-covered sofa below the dais. He too was observing Thalia, but with more of an air of amusement than of lust. He was extremely handsome, with blond curly hair and piercing blue eyes. An elegant moustache drooped about his mouth, which was curved slightly in a cynical smile. His hands, pale as a woman's, glittered with rings and his jacket was of a rich, deep-blue velvet. He was smoking a cigar, turning his head lazily to watch the smoke rings float upwards toward the ceiling.

Thalia tried desperately to communicate to him her fear, hoping that he would approach her so that she could beg him to remove Baron Croydon. But he merely smiled each time she sent him what she considered a pathetically appealing glance. Obviously he enjoyed the sight of a young female in distress.

Indignantly Thalia turned her head about again to gaze upon the empty chair, her cheeks flaming with humiliation and rage.

The painter, ready to begin the finer detail of her face, looked up and exclaimed in disappointment.

"No, no, no!" he cried. "You have lost the mood. You must look mournful, wistful, but not as if you were about to cry."

This was too much for Thalia. It was enough that she was forced to remain still while two odious gentlemen took advantage of her helplessness by ogling her. Now Mr. Rossetti had accused her of being on the verge of tears, as if she would fall prey to such a childish state in such fashionable company.

"I am sorry," she said firmly. "I do not believe I can pose any longer. I am very fatigued and unused to this work." She stood up, putting aside the embroidery thread, and as she felt her hair loose on her back, blushed for shame that the gentlemen were observing her almost in a state of undress. It was little wonder they were staring so; only the most fast type of female would allow any man but her husband to see her with her hair undone. She began to fumble on the floor for the pins. The elegant gentleman who was lounging nearby arose slowly and held out a handful of these articles.

"Allow me, my lady," he said in a soft, low voice, and put up his hands to touch her hair. Thalia trembled again. This was all so ridiculous; she could not object if she were the type of girl he thought her, but as she was Thalia Horrocks, she did.

"You are very kind, sir," she said in a stubborn, small voice. "I can manage on my own."

At that moment, Susannah miraculously drifted out of the crowd and, perceiving Thalia's distress, swiftly helped her to bind up her hair and pin it firmly.

"You wish to leave," she stated calmly. "I will find Lynton and we will go at once."

She left Thalia standing before the impertinent gaze of the languid young man who had assumed his recumbent position upon the sofa, but reappeared in a moment propelling Lynton before her. With a few commanding movements she had retrieved Thalia's cloak from the ground where it had fallen, blocked the path of Baron Croydon, who had excused himself from the lady in red and was bearing down upon Thalia, and turned Lynton and his cousin in the direction of the door.

As they were about to leave the room, Baron Croydon following close behind them, they encountered Lady Guenevere, who was in a heated conversation with Mr. Rossetti.

"Miss Lawrence!" she exclaimed, holding out her lovely hands.

Thalia, who had forgotten her pseudonym, took a moment to respond. "Miss Stillwater has told me about your novel and I shall be glad to aid you. And Mr. Rossetti is insisting that you return so he may finish the picture. Would it be at all possible for you to call upon me, perhaps tomorrow?"

Thalia looked about desperately, and Lady Guenevere, perceiving her troubled gaze and the flushed face of Baron Croydon behind her, quickly added, "It will be a private sitting, my dear. Just you and Susannah and I, and Mr. Rossetti, of course."

Thalia looked at her gratefully. Lady Guenevere smiled in her serene, untroubled way, and Thalia found herself wishing to do anything to accommodate this gracious lady.

"It may be impossible, my lady," she replied with a curtsey, "but I shall endeavour to be here tomorrow. I thank you for your hospitality, and," she turned to Mr. Rossetti, "for your labour in painting my portrait."

"I will be in communication with you next day," Susannah promised Lady Guenevere, also curtseying, and Lynton, who had taken several more glasses of sherry, bent over the lady's hand again, a little more unsteadily than before.

They were once more ushered through the foreboding passage by the absurdly cheerful butler and re-entering their uncomfortable hansom cab, set off into the night. It was not yet late for Susannah and Lynton, who were used to partying until dawn, but Thalia yawned and curled into a small bundle in her comer of the cab, sinking into a comfortable sleep as if nothing had troubled her that night. Susannah smiled fondly at this sight, and Lynton took this opportunity to take possession of one of her hands and gaze soulfully into her eyes, which unfortunately he could barely see in the poor light.

"I have given instructions to the coachman to take Thalia to her home first," he said meaningfully, "and then he shall drive you to your own." Susannah smiled, knowing well that they would pass her house on the way to Thalia's, but not choosing to protest.

They did not speak again, so as not to disturb Thalia, until the cab stopped in Russell Square, whereupon they woke her gently and, after assuring themselves that she had enough presence of mind to slip back into the house unnoticed, Lynton closed the door and they drove off into the night.

Chapter Four

The Further Adventures of Miss Thalia Horrocks in Which
Thalia Receives Three Invitations and an Unexpected Caller

BREAKFAST AT THE HORROCKS household was also taken in the dining room, as it was the only room of admirable proportions and furnishings suitable for this purpose. During the early hours of the day, Mrs. Horrocks permitted the maid to draw aside the heavy crimson draperies, as the sun's rays were then weak and could be trusted not to fade the carpet. But upon this morning there was very little sun at all shining through the Honiton lace undercurtains; Thalia, from her seat facing the windows, could see the dim grey clouds which hovered ominously over the neighbouring rooftops. As Mr. Horrocks was already at his desk in the City, Mrs. Horrocks sat at the head of the table, smiling genially upon her daughters in their matching purple morning costumes.

"There are three letters today," she remarked by way of conversation, "and two are addressed to Thalia."

Thalia, who was feeling remarkably lively considering her late expedition during the night, looked up, startled. The knife which she had been using to butter her toast slipped from her hand and fell upon the tablecloth, leaving a greasy stain.

"Thalia, how can you be so clumsy?" Mrs. Horrocks snapped, gesturing to the maid to dab at the soiled cloth and bring Thalia another knife from the sideboard.

She then picked up the letters beside her on a salver and began to open them with an ornate silver letter opener.

"How very odd," she said. "The script on this letter; it does not look at all familiar. And no number. Merely 'Miss Thalia Horrocks, Russell Square.' One wonders how the messenger found the correct house."

She turned open the invitation inside and read the contents with a frown. Thalia sat quietly like a condemned man.

"Miss Susannah Stillwater," Mrs. Horrocks said, looking up and fixing Thalia with a suspicious stare. "Who is she?" Thalia, now calm in the face of a known adversary, responded to her mother's query in her natural manner. "An acquaintance of Lynton and Letitia Lanston," she lied blithely. "A very amiable girl."

Mrs. Horrocks continued to scrutinize Thalia's features for a few moments, then looked down at the paper in her hand as if it were a loathsome reptile.

"She has a most peculiar script," she commented, "quite an angular style for a female hand, and most plain." She began to read the note aloud in a cold, formal voice.

"'Dear Miss Horrocks, You may not remember me well; I made your acquaintance at the home of your cousin, Mr. Lynton Lanston, whose sister I was visiting. Some friends are coming to my home to drink tea with me today and I would be glad of the pleasure of your company also. Please do not disappoint me.' There is a postscript appended. The young lady mentions that Miss Lanston will also be present." She stared at Thalia again. "What can you have done to bring yourself to the attention of this female?" she asked.

"I was merely pleasant," Thalia replied innocently, "as you have instructed me to be. We had only a few words. I suppose that she remembered me because she is new in town. Her parents are old friends of the Lanstons and they had just moved to London. She is a very timid girl and perhaps hopes to meet some other young ladies in this manner. I would say," she continued in a confiding tone, "that it is her mother who has instructed her to hold such a party, for she is so shy I am sure she would not dare to think of it on her own. Her mother is a very commanding woman, and she seemed to have a strong influence upon her daughter."

"As all mothers should," answered Mrs. Horrocks bluntly. "I do not consider this at all proper as I have not made Mrs. Stillwater's acquaintance. We will put this aside for the moment and look at the others. Ah, this one is definitely from Miss Letitia. She has such beautiful penmanship." She looked pointedly at both of her daughters, who had failed her in this regard. "The Viscountess Lanston requests the pleasure of Miss Thalia Horrocks' company at a Ball, on Wednesday, the tenth of June at ten o'clock," she read.

"There is an R.S.V.P. added." She looked at Thalia, who had been expecting a merely conventional note from her cousin and was glowing at the prospect of attending a real ball. "You must answer this immediately after you have finished breakfast."

"I will, Mama," Thalia answered dutifully, concealing her great excitement about this invitation to such an exclusive gathering. There had been many such when Letty had come out a year ago, but as Mrs. Horrocks had turned them all down, declaring that she did not wish Thalia to associate with those of the frivolous and immoral upper classes, the Lanstons had dropped her from their invitation list. Thalia assumed that her mother was accepting this invitation only to strengthen her disapproval of the one from Susannah.

Flora was becoming more and more petulant as she saw her sister invited to such glamorous and exciting places and spoke up quickly, hoping that the last invitation would include her. "And the other letter, Mama?"

"The other is from Mrs. Cornfield," said Mrs. Horrocks, perusing it rapidly. "It is an invitation to a dinner at her house tomorrow. She requests the presence of myself, Mr. Horrocks, and my two daughters."

"It includes me!" exclaimed Flora excitedly in her high voice. She bounced up and down in her chair. "What shall I wear? I wonder if Mr. Cornfield's brother shall be there?"

"That is a most inappropriate question," answered Mrs. Horrocks primly, folding the letter and putting it back into the envelope. "However, I do believe that he will be, as otherwise Mrs. Cornfield will not have the correct number. As to your clothes, I believe your yellow tarlatan dresses will answer nicely. I do like to see my daughters dressed alike. It precludes jealousy, prevents an ostentatious display—" she inclined her head toward Thalia "—and affirms your relationship as sisters."

As neither girl displayed much filial affection for the other, Mrs. Horrocks felt that an external display of this necessary emotion was required. Flora continued to bounce excitedly up and down but Thalia was preoccupied with other matters.

"And the other invitation, Mama?" she asked. "The one from Miss Stillwater?"

"There is no need to respond to it as there was no R.S.V.P. upon the letter," Mrs. Horrocks said firmly, putting aside the letters and picking up her cup of tea. "It is quite incorrect for you to attend such a gathering until I have met this young lady and her mother and discovered what sort of people they are. I shall send my card along to the address, I believe it is in Belgravia," she said, glancing at the envelope, "and after they have called upon us, perhaps you will be able to accept another such invitation." She smiled at her daughter sweetly with her fixed smile, considering that she had acted very generously indeed in inviting such unknown individuals to call upon her.

Thalia rose from the table hastily, folding her napkin and leaving it beside her plate.

"If I may be excused, Mama?" she asked. "I have finished my breakfast and I would like to reply to Letty—Letitia's invitation."

"Very well," said Mrs. Horrocks, turning to a plate of muffins beside her. "Be certain that you show it to me before it is sent. And Thalia dear, do try to be a little more careful in your penmanship than usual."

"I will, Mama," Thalia promised, running hastily from the room and hurrying up to her bedroom, where she had a small writing desk and a supply of stationery and ink.

She hurriedly scrawled a note to Lynton, explaining the situation and begging for his assistance, and then more laboriously replied to the invitation to the ball, having to start over many times as she misspelt words and left untidy blots of ink all over the paper. The final copy had only one small blot near her signature, and she brought it down to the sitting room where Mrs. Horrocks was sedately working upon her household accounts, while Flora could be heard doing her exercises upon the piano in the drawing room. She was as poor a musician as Thalia, partially because they had both been taught by Miss Mallet, but she was much more ardent in her labours, hoping thereby to catch the eye, or the ear, of Mr. Cornfield's younger brother.

"Very nice, Thalia dear," Mrs. Horrocks said, scanning the letter. "There is an unfortunate blot here—"

"I know, Mama. I am sorry," Thalia interrupted, "but the others were worse."

"Very well then," her mother replied complacently. "I will give it to Joseph to deliver."

"I can bring it to him," Thalia offered eagerly. "It will prevent you from having to disturb your schedule."

"Thank you very much," Mrs. Horrocks said with great surprise. "That is very thoughtful of you, my dear. And then it will be your turn to practice."

"Mama, with your permission," Thalia answered, "I wish to work upon my penmanship. It is sorely in need of improvement."

Mrs. Horrocks was yet more amazed at this request but nodded with great composure, and Thalia exited with a quick curtsey to seek out Joseph. She inserted the note to Lynton into the envelope as she walked and hoped, with some trepidation, that her usually irresponsible cousin would respond quickly to her plea. She then re-entered the house and seated herself again at the desk to begin the writing of her Novel under the guise of penmanship exercises.

This process was a very laborious one indeed. She had first to invent a pseudonym for her Heroine, and taking down the volume of Tennyson poems which Letty had lent to her, she chose the name Mariana. She planned to begin with the childhood of her

Heroine and wished desperately that she had had a chance to question Lady Guenevere, or even Susannah, on the subject. But as the Novel needed to be written immediately, she invented a childhood much like her own in which the Heroine had a dashing and charming father who took her with him everywhere, into gaming houses and brothels and casinos. Thalia could remember vividly the people and sights she had seen in such places and covered many pages with descriptions until she realized that even her own father would hardly have approved of his daughter joining the ranks of the pretty horse-breakers. She decided he must die, but invented a more respectable death than her father's, having the Heroine witness his death of apoplexy in the tenth page. It was a very touching scene; Thalia was certain that it would bring tears to the eyes of her readers. Mariana threw herself upon him as he lay gasping on the drawing-room floor, calling his name repeatedly and wiping his feverish brow, as he died with her name on his lips.

She next had to decide the future of her Heroine, and after a few troubling moments, hit upon the ingenious solution of sending her to live with a horrid old aunt in Bath. Thalia had never been to Bath and took many liberties with her description of this city as her Heroine entered it, but she found great pleasure in creating the character of the odious aunt, whose resemblance to Mrs. Horrocks she steadfastly ignored. Mariana was treated with great cruelty by her elderly relative, who used her as a servant and did not permit her to have any young acquaintances. After many pages of gruesome descriptions in which the Heroine was forced to scrub the kitchen floors and obey the smallest whims of her aunt and disagreeable cousin (who bore a marked similarity to Flora, both in character and appearance), Thalia realized that it was time for Mariana to make her escape. The Heroine accomplished this by slipping out of the house one evening by the kitchen door and taking the train to London. As Thalia knew little of trains, she skipped over the journey rapidly, and soon had her Heroine wandering about the streets of London at night. But what would happen next?

She reread the pages she had just completed but these gave her no clue, and after some time spent in deep concentration, she concluded that she had really learned nothing of the lives of the pretty horsebreakers during her last evening's adventures. She knew well that Mariana could not suddenly set herself up in the style in which Lady Guenevere lived, but what path was taken to achieve such success? She decided with some relief that she could put off the next chapter of the Novel until she had spoken further with Lady Guenevere or Susannah and began to recopy the pages she had already written, attempting to do so without leaving blots upon the paper, but with little success.

As she was so occupied, there was a knock upon her door, and Miss Mallet thrust her head inside, saying in a small timid voice, "Miss Thalia, Mr. Lynton is calling upon you. He is downstairs in the drawing room."

Thalia was as startled as her governess, both by the promptness of his response and by the fact that he had taken the unprecedented step of calling at the Horrocks household. She hid her papers quickly within the desk and, smoothing her dress, followed Miss Mallet down the stairs. Mrs. Horrocks was waiting at the bottom.

"Thalia," she hissed sharply, as her daughter reached the last step. "I do not approve of young gentlemen calling upon my daughters. I do not wish to see him, but send him about his business promptly and inform him, with delicacy I hope, that he is not to call upon us again. Do you understand?"

Thalia nodded compliantly and proceeded towards the drawing room, where Lynton stood gazing at the large ebony clock upon the mantel and fingering his hat nervously. He looked desperately at Miss Mallet as she entered and Thalia responded with the smallest shrug of her shoulders to indicate that she was helpless in the matter.

"How thoughtful of you to call upon me, Lynton," she said pleasantly. "Was there *something* which you wished to discuss?"

Lynton glanced at Miss Mallet, who was sitting on the large sofa, blinking her eyes nervously and patting the cushion next to her to indicate that Thalia should seat herself. Thalia ignored her governess resolutely.

"It is about the invitation from Susann...em...er...Miss Stillwater," Lynton stammered.

"Yes," Thalia murmured conventionally, hoping that he would have the presence of mind to conceal the true facts of their speech.

Lynton thought with great concentration for a few moments and then said, rather stiltedly, "My sister Letitia requested that I inform you that she is planning to attend the—ah—gathering at Susann—Miss Stillwater's home today and hopes that you would come with her." He looked at Miss Mallet and turned his hat about in his hands again. "I might add," he said abruptly, "that I will escort both of you, if you choose, and we will call for you in our carriage."

Thalia smiled approvingly. "I must ask Mama," she said, and left the room quickly. Lynton glanced about desperately in her absence; Miss Mallet stared with much intensity upon the enormous roses in the carpet pattern.

Thalia returned after a long interval, her cheeks flushed and her dark eyes dancing. "Mama has given permission," she exclaimed. "I assured her that Mrs. Stillwater was very respectable indeed and a dear friend of your mother. She is most displeased, but I believe she will allow me to go."

Lynton sighed with relief and, passing his hand over his hair, resettled his hat upon his head and with an elegant bow took his leave of his cousin and her governess. Thalia almost seized Miss Mallet and danced a wild polka with her as he left, but realized immediately the necessity of mollifying her mother and hurried back into the sitting room prepared to stitch upon her seat cover demurely and act the model daughter until such time as the Lanstons would arrive for her.

Mrs. Horrocks was a stern taskmaster throughout the afternoon, searching for the smallest fault in Thalia's behaviour which would enable her to rescind her grudgingly given permission but, to her consternation, Thalia was exemplary in every detail. She was kind to her sister, obedient to Miss Mallet, and dutifully dressed herself for the outing in the brilliant grass-green outfit which her mother knew she abhorred. Mrs. Horrocks was so pleased with her daughter's manners that she graciously deigned to meet Miss Letitia at the door, thankful that Mr. Lynton had obligingly remained in the carriage. She was glad of this opportunity to cross-examine Letitia upon Mrs. Stillwater and her mysterious daughter and, when Thalia descended the stairs, she found Letty in great distress, stumbling over her words and endeavouring to remember the fictitious biography which Lynton had dunned into her.

Chapter Five

*In Which Miss Letitia Lanston Finds Herself in the Home of
a Prominent London Courtesan, Thalia Is Mistaken for
a Pretty Horsebreaker, and Mr. Lanston and Miss Stillwater
Become Better Acquainted*

"I DO NOT RECALL," Letty was saying, her eyes dark with fear. "I believe it is—no, that is to say—"

"What is it you do not recall, Letty?" Thalia demanded, interposing herself between her mother and her terrified cousin.

"What profession Mr. Stillwater is in," Letty stammered.

"Why, he is a barrister, is he not?" Thalia said blithely, certain this would meet with her mother's approval. "He held a position in the country until lately and was just accepted into a London firm. Don't you remember Mrs. Stillwater telling us that, Letty?" she asked encouragingly.

"Oh yes," Letty replied weakly, seeming very unconvinced. "Mrs. Horrocks, you must excuse us," she went on more gracefully, "but we are very late already. I am glad to have had this opportunity to speak with you."

"Thank you, Miss Lanston," Mrs. Horrocks answered formally, impressed as usual by Letitia's pretty manners. "I appreciate your generosity in offering to accompany my daughter."

"It is nothing," Letty murmured, slipping out of the door and almost running towards the carriage through the light rain which was beginning to fall. As soon as her cousin had entered after her and the door was shut, she gazed at Thalia reproachfully and said, "Thalia, how *could* you have placed me in such a position?" Recalling that she was even now on her way to the den of one of the notorious pretty horsebreakers, she added, "How *can* you have asked this of me?"

"It was partially Lynton's idea," Thalia said calmly, glancing at him as she spoke, but he gave no sign of having heard her words as he was gazing out of the carriage window with a silly smile upon his face. Thalia turned away from him and back to Letty.

"Letty, I assure you," she said warmly, "that Susannah is very respectable. She is a woman like you or me." Seeing that Letty blushed at this, she cast about for other reassurances. "I vow to you Letty that as soon as we enter the house to which we are going—has Lynton told you of Lady Guenevere?" Letty nodded timidly. "I promise you," Thalia continued, "that you will be given a small sitting room to yourself where no one will disturb you. I see you brought your needlework," she said, espying Letty's ivory workbasket beside her on the seat. "That will help you pass the time." Thalia would not have thought it possible but Letty looked more sorrowful than before; however, further conversation was difficult due to the rattle of the carriage wheels upon the cobblestones. Instead, the three sat lost in their own thoughts. Letty stared at her hands as if hoping to derive some courage thereby which would bolster her during her forthcoming ordeal, Lynton continued to gaze raptly out the window (although little could be seen due to the thickening rain), while Thalia reviewed the questions she must ask of Lady Guenevere.

By the time they had arrived at Miss Stillwater's residence the summer rain was pouring down and distant thunder could be heard. Lynton sprang out of the carriage as if he had been shot from a cannon and bowled along the pathway to the house, returning a short time later with Susannah, who had covered her golden curls with a brilliant crimson cloak. Her eyes were glowing warmly, her cheeks were rosy, it seemed almost (as Lynton pointed out earnestly) as if the sun had condescended to enter the carriage. Susannah greeted Thalia fondly and introduced herself to Letty, apologizing for having drawn her into this adventure but explaining that it was the only method she could contrive for removing Thalia from her mother's supervision.

Letty, although she remained reserved, said thoughtfully that she understood. She was feeling very out of place, as if she were at a party to which she had not been invited. Thalia was relating to Susannah eagerly the amusing stories she had invented about Mrs. Stillwater and her daughter, and Lynton gazed at Susannah worshipfully, interrupting to ply her with compliments upon her wit and cleverness. Letty saw immediately that her brother was infatuated with the beautiful girl and trembled as a premonition of great trouble came over her. She saw that Lynton and Susannah were far more deeply involved with each other than either suspected. Letty thought with a sigh of the serene afternoon she had planned for herself, working upon her embroidery and perhaps visiting Mr. Crofts, the tutor of her younger brothers. Instead, she was embroiled in this web of intrigues and passions, and felt sadly out of her depth.

There were only a few short blocks between Susannah's villa and the residence of Lady Guenevere. As the carriage rolled to a stop before the front door, the other three piled out, giggling like children and prancing about in the rain, before they dashed into the house. Letty, feeling even more unwanted than before, followed sedately, clasping her workbox tightly in one hand.

She was overwhelmed by the passageway and stood looking about with wide eyes, while the others seemed unaffected by its Gothic gloominess. Thalia chattered with the friendly butler, Lynton feinted playfully with the suit of armour in the corner, and Susannah poked her fingers at the irritated owl whose name, she declared, was Horatio.

Letty was brought up short again at the threshold of the drawing room. It was very strange, unlike any she had ever seen, with a huge fire blazing upon the hearth and the tapestries upon the walls quivering slightly with the draught. The heavy draperies at the windows were drawn aside to allow a little of the light from outside to sweep across the plain polished furniture and bowls of flowers. At one end Letty saw what she thought at first must be a picture. A beautiful woman in an amber gown, like those of the Middle Ages, was embroidering upon a scene of glowing colours. As Letty stared at her, she came to life, rising gracefully to meet her guests.

"Welcome," she said dramatically as she swept down upon them. "Miss Thalia Lawrence." Letty blushed as she recalled that she had helped Thalia invent this pseudonym. "And Susannah, my dear." She embraced Miss Stillwater. "And the charming Mr. Lanston." With amazement, Letty saw her brother go down on one knee and press a fervent kiss upon the Lady's hand.

"And this of course must be your sister," Lady Guenevere said, turning to Letty and extending her hand. Lynton was confounded for he saw nothing of similarity between his fairness and blue eyes and Letty's brown hair and grey eyes, but Lady Guenevere had noted the same oval facial structure, the same straight nose and the same calm smile.

"Miss Letitia Lanston," said Letty, averting her eyes, but feeling Lady Guenevere clasp her hand warmly she looked up and perceived that the Lady was gazing at her with an expression of great concern and understanding. Her words underscored this impression.

"If there is anything I can do to make you feel at home," Lady Guenevere said graciously.

"There is," Thalia spoke up quickly, recalling her promise to Letty, but she was interrupted by Mr. Rossetti who had broken away from his canvas and was standing some three feet from her, staring at her aghast "Why, where is the charming dress of last night?" he demanded. "How can you degrade your beauty by appearing in such a hideous outfit?"

"It was not my dress," Thalia apologized sorrowfully, with a little glance at Letty. In truth, she had hidden it beneath her mattress as soon as she had arrived home. "This is my mother's favourite costume. I wore it to please her." Mr. Rossetti shook his head in amazement that any mother could take pride in a daughter dressed in yards of a brilliant green watered silk, trimmed with black fringe and jet buttons.

"It will not do," he said firmly. "Lady Guenevere, you must find something from your own wardrobe for this girl. I will not be able to continue if I am forced to look upon that odious colour!" He turned abruptly and stalked back to his canvas.

Thalia was about to protest that Lady Guenevere should not do so, that indeed none of her clothes would fit Thalia, but the lady smiled, amused by the painter's demand, and said gently, "He is quite right. Come with me, Thalia dear." She turned to the others. "We will be but a moment."

Thalia followed her meekly up the grand stairway to the largest bedroom, which was decorated in the same Gothic manner as the remainder of the house. The bed was of dark oak, hung with linen curtains embroidered with fantastic animals and flowers. Two stained glass windows shone sullenly, as a result of the grey-ness outside, as if they were muted jewels. Huge white lilies flowered in burnished copper pots on the floor; to one side stood an oak wardrobe which had been painted with medieval scenes done in golds, scarlets, emeralds, and sapphires.

The dresses inside the wardrobe glowed in the same gemlike hues. They were loosely constructed, unlike the ordinary dresses of the period, which were fitted to the wearer's body like a glove. Lady Guenevere chose a velvet gown of the same shade of old ivory as Thalia had worn the night before, and, with the aid of her French maid, Thalia was divested of her green dress and the cage-like crinoline and immersed in the folds of the ivory velvet.

Rummaging through a silver casket, glittering with jewels, Lady Guenevere picked out a belt of gold and emeralds and fitted it snugly beneath Thalia's breasts. The extra fullness of the dress had been gathered backwards so that it fell from the belt in a train and swept the floor as she walked.

"These are not real," Thalia gasped.

"I had my jewellery reset into these belts," Lady Guenevere said calmly, holding up a handful of silver and rubies, gold and topazes. "It was of little use to me in the former settings."

Thalia gazed down open-mouthed at the emeralds shining about her waist as the maid gently removed the pins from her hair and combed it out to a full, rich mane of curls. At length Lady Guenevere led Thalia to a tall mirror behind a fringed curtain, and Thalia became so entranced by the vision of herself in the glass that the lady also had to lead her gently away and back down the stairs.

As they entered the drawing room, Thalia saw with remorse that she had left Letitia quite alone and helpless, and she whispered to Lady Guenevere that she must find her a private sitting room to work in. Susannah and Lynton had helped themselves to some brandy from the side table and were standing before the fire with their glasses, engrossed in what seemed a very amusing conversation. The painter was busy about his work at the end of the room. Letty sat self-consciously upon a sofa, looking like an orphan in her dove grey merino dress, ornamented only with pearl buttons and lace at the collar and cuffs.

She glanced up as Lady Guenevere and Thalia entered the room and stared at her cousin in amazement, at first taken aback by the strangeness of her attire, but slowly realizing how it suited Thalia's beauty. She glowed like a candle, the rich ivory colour a perfect foil to her dark curls and flushed cheeks. Mr. Rossetti was also spellbound by Thalia; he led her silently and gently to her seat upon the dais, and Thalia re-created effortlessly the pose which she had learned the night before.

Letty crept up to look at the half-completed picture and was pleased by the richness of the colours and the superb design. She herself had a superior aesthetic sense; she was an excellent musician and created her own embroidery designs of appealing proportions. She recognized with some surprise the enormous talents of this strange painter and of Lady Guenevere, who had collected so much beauty about her. She also acknowledged with a gasp her admiration of Thalia's natural adaptation to her pose. Hearing her indrawn breath, the painter turned to her and said proudly, "She would be an excellent actress."

"Oh no!" cried Letty involuntarily, for to say a girl was an actress was the same as saying she was a lewd woman.

"Actresses are artists also," Mr. Rossetti said sharply, and Letty, feeling herself rebuked, was about to turn and leave, when she heard Lady Guenevere say softly behind her, "It is not the girl's fault. She can never have seen a play in a theatre."

The painter admitted this truth with a little nod of his head and Lady Guenevere took Letty's hand, saying, "I shall bring you to a sitting room which you will have all to yourself."

As they passed Lynton and Susannah, who were still laughing merrily, Susannah called out, "Lady Guenevere, I have been promising Lynton a tour of your home. May we have your permission?"

"Certainly," Lady Guenevere replied with an amused smile for Susannah and the handsome young man beside her.

She and Letty proceeded down the ghostly passage which became more friendly as one reached the back of the house, being cluttered with cupboards full of strange blue and white china and vases of peacock feathers, rather than owls and knights in full armour. Opening a small door, Lady Guenevere showed Letty into the most beautiful room she had ever seen in her life. It was done completely in shades of green; the curtains at the windows were tapestries of hunting scenes; the fire screen and chairs and sofas were covered with beautiful needlework. A small bright fire burned on the hearth and a canary sang from a golden cage. Letty, forgetting her shyness, flew about the room in wonder. Everywhere she found the most beautiful embroidery designs she had ever imagined. Upon the fire screen was a huge tree, filled with squirrels and birds of all descriptions and even a smug-looking cat. The back of the sofa had been stitched to represent a wild garden, tangled with herbs and wonderful flowers, with small snails and bright butterflies peering out from amongst them. Each seat cover had its own floral design, simple depictions of lilies and roses and daffodils. Letty turned about and said with awe, "Is this your work?"

Lady Guenevere nodded, flattered by the young girl's obvious delight.

Letty sat down breathlessly upon the sofa. "It is incredible," she said softly. "How can you ever have learned this? How can you ever have done it all?"

"It is my passion," the lady replied simply, seating herself on the sofa across from Letty. "My first attempts were very crude. You see some of them upon the walls," she indicated with her hand the framed samplers and brightly-coloured scenes hung about the room. "But I redecorate my house often and as I require completely new furnishings I have quite a lot of practice. And now I notice that you have brought with you your workbox. Show me some of your own needlework."

With embarrassment, Letty pulled out the seat cover upon which she was working but Lady Guenevere praised the design highly, declaring that she herself could not have conceived of such a handsome pattern.

"I notice that you are trying to create the impression that this leaf is leaning out towards the viewer," she said, holding up the piece for Letty's shy nod. "I have a stitch which I just invented a few months ago that will give you exactly that effect. Let me teach it to you." She opened the mahogany work case beside her and, drawing out an embroidery needle and thread of a darker shade of green, proceeded to demonstrate the stitch to Letty.

Soon she had taught her several new techniques and Letty was dutifully practicing them, showing the results every now and then for Lady Guenevere's approval. A timid little maid brought in a tea service consisting of a strange Japanese teapot with equally odd cups. The two needlewomen put aside their work and were soon gossiping with each other. Letty found, to her great surprise, that she was confessing to Lady Guenevere her admiration for the tutor of her younger brothers, one Mr. Edward Crofts, and stopped in some embarrassment.

Lady Guenevere pretended not to notice, pressing upon Letty some of the delicious warm scones and saying, "He sounds like a very fine young man indeed. It is rare that one meets a man of equal charm and intelligence. If he is as brilliant as you believe, why does he not begin his own academy for young gentlemen? I am certain that he would be a refreshing change from the brutal old men who usually run such schools."

"Why we have never..." Letty began, "that is to say, I am certain the idea has never occurred to him. But of course it would require a great deal of money. Still I am sure that it would be exactly what he would most love to do." She looked at Lady Guenevere with admiration. "I shall suggest it to him this evening," she said, "but I will thank you in advance for I am certain he will do so when he hears your suggestion." She thought a little sorrowfully to herself that if Edward could find the money to begin a school, he would be lost to her forever. Perceiving her sadness, Lady Guenevere brought the conversation around to Thalia, and Letty began to smile again, relating all of the various schemes Thalia had embarked upon since childhood. As she did not know what sort of autobiography Thalia had invented to accompany her pseudonym, she avoided referring to her as her cousin, merely explaining their close relationship by saying that their mothers had been good friends in childhood.

"I do hope she writes this novel," Letty said wistfully, "for so many of her other plans have come to nought and she deserves more happiness than she has in her life."

At the moment, the individual in question stuck her head in through the doorway and, smiling engagingly, said, "Oh Lady Guenevere, I am searching for you. Mr. Rossetti has given me a respite and there are some questions I must ask you as you are the Heroine of my Novel."

The Lady smiled and excused herself after Letty had convinced her that she would be quite content alone in the little room working upon her embroidery.

"We will talk in the library, where we shall not be disturbed," said Lady Guenevere to Thalia, opening another doorway off the passage and revealing a large room with a high, vaulted ceiling. The room glowed with colour from the bindings of the many books on the floor-to-ceiling shelves and from the stained glass panels set into a bay window upon one end. Seating Thalia behind the huge desk with paper and pen, Lady Guenevere took a seat opposite her for the interview.

Thalia revealed eagerly the plot of her Novel so far; Lady Guenevere was charmed by the ingenuous manner in which the young girl had used her own experiences.

"But," said Thalia mournfully, as she came to the end of her tale, "I do not know what will happen next. Susannah would not tell me anything of her life; I am sure she was trying to protect my innocence and I fear you will do the same. If I am to write this Novel, I must know exactly the details of your life."

"I will be truthful with you," said Lady Guenevere calmly. "You are not a child but a young woman and deserve to be treated as such. But I must warn you that some details are very unpleasant. I will tell you the complete story, but for your novel you must choose the brighter things as no one likes to read of misery except when it is told by such a master storyteller as Mr. Dickens."

She began to relate slowly to Thalia the story of her life, omitting none of the details which Susannah might have censored: the abject poverty of her childhood as the illegitimate daughter of a poor seamstress, her first working days in a millinery store where she envied the beautifully dressed women and first noticed the appreciative stares of the gentlemen, her eager acceptance of a proposition by one of these men and the brutal reality of his treatment of her and his subsequent desertion when she found she was with child.

"That was my first daughter," she said sadly. "I gave her to my sister to be reared. She is married now to a butcher in Fairbourne. I later had a second daughter but I gave her up to her father, whose wife took her in as her own child. It is terribly sad to have lost a daughter forever."

"You do not know her whereabouts?" asked Thalia, alert to the possibilities of using this information in her Novel.

"No," replied Lady Guenevere sadly. "I never saw her father again, although we were — good friends. He was perhaps the only man I have loved. When he died some years later, his wife disappeared. I tried to trace her for months but she had totally vanished. I guess she had gone off to live in some small country town. And what use would it be to find the child? To tell her that the mother she revered as her own had adopted her and that a stranger who had cast her off was her true mother?"

Thalia reflected wryly that if the mother in question had been Mrs. Horrocks the daughter would undoubtedly be delighted but did not reveal this treacherous thought.

Lady Guenevere continued philosophically, "I did not mind at the time, as I was very ambitious and could not be bothered with children. I knew that money was the key to happiness—but I am digressing from my story."

She went on to explain how she had learned to become selective about the men to whom she granted her favours and how she educated herself laboriously, teaching herself to read and write and then devouring every piece of written material in her vicinity.

"You see the results of my collecting," said Lady Guenevere, glancing about at the book-filled shelves. "I read at first without discrimination, anything I could seize upon, and they are all here, sentimental novels, books of philosophy, erotic literature." Thalia looked about surreptitiously, trying to discover some of the latter.

"That is almost the end of my story," said Lady Guenevere quietly, settling her beautiful white hands in her lap. "I soon found a protector who set me up in my own house in Mayfair. Many years later, another man built me this villa. At times, I was the mistress of only one man (if he was wealthy enough); at other times, I had many callers, as Susannah does now. I must confess that I once married an elderly Peer of the Realm, more in the desire to acquire a title than to be his wife. But I cared for him with kindness until his death a year later. And gradually I gathered about myself the people who interested me—painters such as Mr. Rossetti, and poets, people with amusing conversation and faultless manners and beautiful appearances, so that I can live always surrounded by loveliness and intelligence. It is a rare accomplishment these days; one that is no longer held in acclaim," she said, shaking her head and thinking of the much praised crudeness of Skittles and her sisters.

Thalia did not know exactly what she was expected to say at the end of this story and so begged for some specific advice about which path her Heroine should take next.

After a few suggestions, Lady Guenevere left her scribbling away upon the paper, saying that she must go look for Mr. Rossetti.

Thalia wrote for some time, having Mariana acquire a position as a milliner's assistant, using the information which Lady Guenevere had given her, and even duplicating that Lady's first experience with a man. But she soon tired of this and went in search of her cousin to assure herself that Letty was at ease.

She found her even more settled than she had expected, and her cousin eagerly began to show her the new stitches which she had learned, and to lead her about the room pointing out the artistry in the many fine pieces of embroidery. Thalia, who had little artistic judgement, did not appreciate these, and was murmuring faint praises when she heard an unfamiliar voice saying in honeyed tones, "What good fortune to find two such charming ladies alone."

Whirling about quickly, Thalia saw that it was the languid young blond-haired gentleman of the night before, and seeing that he had mistaken her and Letty for women of loose morals, she determined to protect her cousin at all costs.

"Why, sir," she cried out flirtatiously, "you cannot guess how I have been longing to speak with you. But it is on a private topic. If you will excuse me," she nodded to Letty and, slipping her arm familiarly in his, propelled him out of the room. Letty looked on with amazement but decided that he was merely one of the many strange acquaintances Thalia had met recently and settled down again to her needlework.

The young man was charmed by Thalia's acquiescence and the coquettish looks she was sending him from beneath her fluttering dark lashes.

"Lord Eustace Parringdon, at your command, fair lady, or should I say, dark lady?" he remarked, slipping his arm about Thalia's waist.

"Miss Thalia Lawrence," Thalia replied boldly, striving to retain her composure. No man had ever put his arm about her before and she was discomfited by the strange feeling of closeness. She could feel his warm body pressed against her own, yet she could not move away for he would know she was not what she feigned to be.

"I am delighted to make your acquaintance, Lord Parringdon," she said seductively.

"Stacey, to my friends," he responded quickly, with a provocative pressure of his hand upon her body, "and I am certain that you are going to be one of my friends."

He halted abruptly in their stroll down the passageway and putting his arms about her, pressed a kiss into her dark curls and then upon her lips. Thalia tried to respond as she imagined a pretty horsebreaker would and found to her surprise that it was really very pleasant. She placed her arms about his back, stroking the nape of his neck fondly, and allowing her lips to part slightly beneath his. However, just as she was beginning to enjoy herself, his embraces became more ardent and he began to kiss her wildly about the neck and down the décolletage of her dress, while his hand roved over her thighs beneath the soft velvet. Thinking quickly, Thalia reached back with her foot and tipped over a copper vase filled with peacock feathers which had been placed upon the floor. It fell with a loud clang, and Stacey let her go abruptly, glancing around startled.

"Oh," cried Thalia, looking at him with pretended sorrow, "my dress must have caused it to fall." They both bent to gather up the feathers as Lady Guenevere, alerted by the noise, came out from the drawing room.

"Thalia," she said, looking earnestly first at the girl and then at Eustace Parringdon, "I was about to come in search of you. Mr. Rossetti requires you to model for him again." Eagerly Thalia hurried towards the drawing room, while Stacey followed close behind, murmuring in her ear, "How unfortunate for us, my pretty darling. You must allow me to follow up this charming encounter." He entered the drawing room with her and, as she took up her pose once more, lounged again on the small sofa, sipping from a glass of brandy and staring at Thalia appreciatively. Thalia found to her relief that she was able to maintain her composure, as she did not wish Lady Guenevere to know of the deception which she had practiced upon the young man. Lady Guenevere was also sitting for Mr. Rossetti and she and the painter and the young man soon began a conversation about Art which left Thalia far behind, as they were scornfully denigrating the works shown at the Royal Academy Exhibition and praising the Pre-Raphaelites instead. Thalia became so bored that she was grateful when Susannah and Lynton entered the room hand-in-hand and broke off the conversation by saying that it was time to leave.

"I am afraid the tea party to which you were invited should be long over," said Susannah, her eyes sparkling. "We must take Cinderella home before her wicked stepmother discovers that she is missing."

Thalia wondered for a moment why Susannah and Lynton had been such a long time in exploring the house and why they appeared so pleased with each other, but she put the thought aside and hurried upstairs to exchange regretfully her velvet gown for the hideous green dress. She went to fetch Letty from the sitting room and was relieved to discover when she returned to the rest of the party that Lord Parringdon had disappeared.

The farewells were long and genuine. Letty was grieved that she could no longer learn from Lady Guenevere and distressed that it would not be appropriate for her to call again at this house, but the lady insisted that she should return. Mr. Rossetti demanded that Thalia sit for him one more time so that he could finish the finer details of her features and Thalia begged Lady Guenevere for another conference upon the subject of her Novel.

When they were at last in the carriage, driving through the rain-washed streets, there was yet another goodbye at Susannah's house. Letty had retrieved her usual self-assurance and said with real conviction that she had been glad to meet Miss Stillwater. Lynton found it necessary to escort her inside her house and did not return for many minutes.

Finally, they arrived in Russell Square, where Thalia, not knowing when she would be able to escape from her home again, behaved as if she would not see her cousins until the night of the ball and plied Letty with many questions upon the people who would be present and the dress she was planning to wear.

After she had scurried inside, gleefully allowing the skirts of the green dress to drag through the water and mud of the street, the Lanstons returned home without further conversation, Lynton whistling an absurdly cheerful tune and Letty glowing with the pleasure of revealing the scheme about the boys' academy to Mr. Crofts.

Chapter Six

*In Which the Reader Makes the Acquaintance of the Odious
Mr. Frederic Cornfield and His Equally Odious Mama*

THALIA SPENT THE FOLLOWING day in quiet pursuits, playing
a little upon the piano, submitting to the unusual torture of a bath
in preparation for the forthcoming dinner at the Cornfields, and
finally slipping away to continue her penmanship exercises.

She wrote quite a few more chapters of her Novel that
afternoon, for she had decided that her Heroine would find herself
in an Interesting Condition as a result of her first seduction and
would give up her baby to a stranger on the streets. This was a
very pathetic little scene in which Mariana sobbed in a heart-
rending manner while her infant daughter was borne away from
her and disappeared into the London fog, but Thalia considered
this not only artistic but clever for at any time when the action of
the book began to lag she could have the child, now grown into a
beautiful young girl, reappear and throw herself into her mother's
arms.

Next the Heroine found herself a handsome and dashing
Protector, modelled somewhat after Lord Parringdon. He set her
up in a charming bower in St. John's Wood and Thalia found great
delight in categorizing all the details of this love nest, for it was
very much like her own ideal household. At once Thalia realized

that the course of events was running too smoothly and accordingly introduced a villain, the evil Baron Crofton, who strangely resembled Baron Croydon. Thalia liberally interpreted the remarks which Susannah had made about the baron and had her baron use Mariana brutally. She found it very easy to avoid the details of the more intimate scenes, for she merely stated that the baron and Mariana entered the bedroom and then began the next sentence with his leaving the house, continuing with several passages on Mariana's grief and shame.

As she was deeply engrossed in this fascinating drama, there was a knock upon the door and her mother demanded sharply if she had dressed yet for the dinner. "Remember, the yellow tarlatan," she said imperiously. "I will send Betty to you as soon as she has finished with my hair."

Thalia reluctantly hid the new pages of the manuscript beneath her mattress, next to Letty's crumpled dress, and applied herself to the laborious chore of struggling into her largest crinoline, the only one which could support the enormous skirts of the yellow tarlatan.

The dress itself was an extremely close fit, with rows of tiny buttons down the back, and Thalia was glad of Betty's presence when the maid at last entered the room and helped her into it.

"Your mama has said you are to wear your coral necklace," the maid commented as the buttons were finished and the huge skirts, trimmed with yards of pink satin ruching, were adjusted over the frame of the crinoline.

Thalia found the necklace in her small jewellery box lying forlorn with the few pieces of jewellery her mother considered it appropriate for a young girl to own: a pearl necklace and a cameo brooch edged with seed pearls. Thalia sighed, thinking of Lady Guenevere's belt of gold and emeralds, while Betty fastened the necklace for her and pinned back her hair into a smooth chignon.

"And you are to wear your dark blue cloak and new bonnet, miss," the maid said in a few minutes, stepping back to survey her work. With a gasp, Thalia realized that she had not seen the bonnet since her night at Cremorne Gardens. She could not remember if Susannah had taken it as she had promised or whether it had simply been left behind in the cab. With Betty's competent aid, she pretended to make a thorough search for the hat, knowing all the while that it would not be found, and therefore descended quite late down the passage to where the rest of the family awaited her. Mr. Horrocks was attired in his favourite hound's-tooth-checked jacket, with a vivid yellow vest and his heaviest gold watch chain; his wife was dressed in her usual mousseline purple evening gown, and Flora looked a miniature replica of Thalia: yellow dress, dark blue cloak, and coral necklace, except that she wore the fashionable pork-pie hat perched above her chignon, the white feather waving gaily as she turned about.

"Thalia, where is your hat? You have made us late already," Mrs. Horrocks snapped.

"I cannot find it, Mama," Thalia replied dutifully. "Betty and I have searched the entire room." She paused and added in dramatic tones, "I fear it must have been stolen."

"Ridiculous!" stated Mrs. Horrocks. "What sort of person would enter a house and take only a hat?"

"A female thief," suggested Thalia helpfully, but her mother did not find this sally amusing.

"If you cannot find it," she declared, "Flora must change into her satin hat with the blue ribbons, and you into yours, Thalia. And quickly."

"But, Mama," Flora wailed, thinking that the younger Mr. Cornfield would not even glance at her in such a sadly out-of-date bonnet.

"Enough," grunted Mr. Horrocks, tapping his cane upon the floor. "Do as your mother has said."

Within a few moments, both girls reappeared crowned by the old-fashioned satin bonnets, and the family entered the carriage to drive around the corner to the Cornfield residence. This was another imposing middle-class mansion, although decorated with a much more gaudy taste than Mrs. Horrocks' home. The passage-way was garishly paved with many-coloured marble stones and a huge gas chandelier cast its harsh light down upon them. From thence, they were ushered into the drawing room which was papered in a blazing wallpaper of crimsons and oranges, obscured

partially by the scores of oil paintings, engravings, and daguerreo-
types of the Cornfield family hung upon it. A huge pier glass over
the mantel threw back the blinding colours, as did the prisms
dangling from the sconces upon the walls. The sofas and draperies
were of flaming scarlet, doing little justice to the poor complexions
of those members of the Cornfield family ranged about the room.

Mr. Cornfield was a pleasant if ineffectual man with thick
brown sideburns and a curling moustache. Frederic, who was
sitting uncomfortably upon a small chair, rose awkwardly as they
came in, looking very ill at ease in a tightly fitting bright blue coat
and trousers trimmed with gold braid. He craned his neck against
his tight collar, thrusting out his prominent Adam's apple in the
process. Thalia tried to avoid his glance and instead greeted his
younger brother, who looked a little more subdued in a tweed
jacket. Flora, angry that her sister had usurped her right to Mr.
Thomas Cornfield, went over to greet Frederic, pumping his hand
rapidly and telling him how handsome he looked.

Meanwhile Mrs. Cornfield had fallen upon her "dearest friend,
Mrs. Horrocks," as she declared in a loud, effusive voice. She was
a large, overblown woman with a florid complexion and she
certainly did not look her best in the scarlet gown, which she had
undoubtedly chosen to match her furnishings. Her fading blond
hair was pulled back untidily into a large knot on her head. She
looked exactly like a fishwife, Thalia thought glumly as she sat
down upon the sofa beside Mr. Cornfield, as far from Frederic as
was possible. However, that irrepressible young man instantly
detached himself from the feeble attempts at conversation which
Flora was making and took up a position behind Thalia, leaning
over the back of the sofa to tell her that she looked "awfully pretty,
if you know what I mean."

Thalia pretended not to know what he meant and instead
queried Mr. Cornfield upon his business. As Mr. Cornfield was the
more inept partner of a flourishing wholesale firm, he could think
of no facts which would be interesting to a young girl, and instead
turned her over to his son, saying, "I know you young people
would rather speak to each other than to an old codger like me."
He departed abruptly to join his wife, who was conducting Mr. and

Mrs. Horrocks upon a tour of the room, showing off the quaint carved lava figurines, the strange crystal spheres, and the brightly coloured enamel depictions of Italian scenes which she had acquired since their previous visit.

Flora had attached herself to Thomas Cornfield, who was an extremely taciturn young man, more interested in carriages and machinery than he was in conversing with a dowdy young miss. He grunted sullenly to all of Flora's dazzling conversational gambits, while Thalia, listening to the earnest outpourings of Frederic, wished that Thomas was the older son.

She attempted to keep her gaze fixed straight ahead and merely nodded to his comments, as Frederic had a particularly foul breath, as well as a most unpleasant face with a spotty complexion and teeth which protruded in front like those of a horse.

"That necklace looks so well upon your neck," he was saying awkwardly, feeling with his grubby hand for her own, which she promptly placed in her lap. "I like your hat," he added lamely.

"It's sadly out of date," Thalia responded coolly.

Feeling at a loss upon the subject of female clothing, Mr. Cornfield proceeded to discourse upon his own. "My mama just ordered this jacket and trousers for me," he said proudly. "Do you like it? She has amazingly good taste. She has picked out my clothes for me since I was a child."

Thalia glanced about the shimmering crimson room contemptuously and then sideways at the tightly fitting jacket which could not disguise the unsightly bulges of Frederic's plump body.

"She has abominable taste," Thalia uttered sweetly.

Mr. Cornfield was a rather amiable young man except upon the subject of his mother whom he revered.

"How can you be expected to recognize good taste?" he demanded haughtily. "Your mother only buys from second-rate merchants to save her precious pennies, as my mama has told me."

"I have friends of impeccable breeding," Thalia replied icily, "whom you would not even know, they are so far above your rank. For instance, have you heard of the Pre-Raphaelite painters?" She was proud to remember this difficult word and glared upon him, willing in the triumph of the moment to stare into his fish-like blue eyes.

"Do they exhibit at the Royal Academy?" Frederic stammered, at a loss for words.

"Of course they don't," Thalia replied imperiously. "Their work is too excellent in quality to be demeaned by hanging it among those cheap melodramatic pictures," she said, trying desperately to recall the conversation she had heard at Lady Guenevere's but proud of the quelling effect which her words appeared to have on Mr. Cornfield. As he was struggling to frame a suitable reply, the extremely officious butler entered the room to announce that dinner was served. Mr. Cornfield escorted Mrs. Horrocks, while Mrs. Cornfield declared in her strident voice that Frederic was to take in Thalia, and Thomas to take in Flora, while she brought up the rear with Mr. Horrocks.

It was as Thalia had feared: she was seated beside Frederic throughout the dinner, giving her a superb chance to watch his clumsy table manners as he gobbled the soup and dripped gravy down the front of his new jacket. Fortunately the Horrockses did not approve of their daughters' entering into the conversation overly much, even when at a formal dinner, and the adults chattered away about business concerns, the weather, and politics, leaving three of the young people to complete their dinner in silence. Frederic, however, interrupted often to voice his opinions upon the subjects they discussed, but even his doting mother frowned at him, for he usually burst out with a statement in the middle of one of Mr. Horrocks' long and halting discourses.

At last the dreadful meal was over; the roast had been overdone, the cream sauce had curdled and there was an excessive amount of salt in the soup. As Mrs. Cornfield had devoured her meal with obvious relish, as did all the Cornfields, Thalia could only assume that she did not recognize the lack of talent in her own kitchen.

The entire party trooped back into the drawing room, since Mrs. Cornfield did not believe in the convention of the gentlemen remaining behind to drink their port in peace. "They only get tipsy, you know," she remarked archly, "without us women about to look after them."

She was turning to indicate to the others the seats they should take, when she saw Mrs. Horrocks' speculative gaze upon Frederic, who was standing beside Thalia.

"Oh, Thalia," she declared in a meaningful voice, with a wink at Mrs. Horrocks, "I have just acquired the sheet music for the most charming song which you must try upon the piano but I have left it in the back sitting room. Freddy, go along and help her look for it."

Flora looked sullen at this, wishing there was some excuse made for her to leave the room with the younger Mr. Cornfield, who had seated himself stolidly upon a small chair away from the others.

Thalia, however, was chagrined and swept out of the room as swiftly as possible, hoping to race to the sitting room and return with the music before Frederic could reach her, but she had not counted upon the speed which desire had lent to his feet, and she found herself trapped in a corner of the dim sitting room, where only one light was burning, unable to avoid his groping hands.

"Thalia, Thalia," he was muttering hoarsely, fixing her with his glittering, prominent blue eyes while his hands roved over her bodice. "You don't know how I have been waiting for this moment."

"I only know that I am here to look for some music," she said frigidly, trying to fend him off with her hands but finding herself pressed against the wall by the superior weight of his stout, sweaty body. He tried to plant a kiss upon her lips but missed, and instead his moist lips landed, partly on, partly off her nose.

"Freddy," cried Thalia, becoming a little desperate and using his mother's name for him in the hopes that it would bring him to his senses, but it only encouraged him the more.

"I knew that you thought fondly of me," he said triumphantly, taking a firmer grasp of her waist with his perspiring hands and making another attempt for her lips. As Thalia began to turn her head from side to side, this was quite a struggle, until at last his efforts were successful and he caught her full-mouth. His lips beneath hers were moist and fleshy, not at all like the lips of Lord Parringdon, and as he was not at all an experienced kisser, he pressed his mouth so firmly against hers that her teeth cut into her cheeks from the inside until she felt that her mouth was so bruised that she would never be able to kiss anyone again.

Fortunately at that moment Mrs. Cornfield's ebullient voice was heard calling in the passageway, "Oh, children! What is taking you so long?" She was so used to browbeating her son that she could not even let him alone for a few moments but had come along to see if she could aid in his seduction of Thalia.

"Oh," she said coyly as she entered the room. "It is just as I thought. You do make such a charming couple. Thalia is the ideal height for you, Freddy."

Frederic had let loose of Thalia when he heard his mother's voice and she now pushed him aside, marching to the centre of the room and saying, "Where is the music you wanted, Mrs. Cornfield?"

"Oh, you'll never guess," Frederic's mother replied with a simpering smile. "It was in the drawing room all along. But these things do work out for the best, as it has given you and Freddy a chance to become better acquainted."

She put her arm about her son fondly and led him back to the other room, while Thalia trailed miserably behind, contemplating for a moment bolting out the front door and running back to Russell Square.

As she entered the drawing room, her tongue feeling about the inside of her mouth for the bruised spots, her mother looked up pleasantly with a complacent smile upon her face and Thalia cursed the whims of a morality which would not permit her even to have gentlemen callers with Miss Mallet present but would affectionately condemn her to be trapped in a dark room with such an unprincipled young man as Frederic Cornfield.

As Freddy had taken a seat near his mother on the sofa, Thalia plopped down upon a chair ungracefully, bringing a small warning frown from her mother.

"Thalia, dear, your mother and I have thought of the nicest surprise for you," Mrs. Cornfield was calling out in a sing-song way. "Your mama was telling me that she did not know how you were to go to your cousin Letitia's ball, as she herself does not wish to go—well, you know why," she said, casting an apologetic glance at Mrs. Horrocks, who was alarmed that her private family matters were about to be aired in public. "And Miss Mallet would not be a suitable escort, for of course she is not of the proper station to be a chaperone at such a fashionable gathering. Well, you will never conceive of the brilliant manner in which we solved this little—er—problem, shall we call it."

Thalia could not indeed think of the solution, as she had not until this moment considered it a problem. She waited resignedly for Mrs. Cornfield's next words.

"Why it is as plain as the nose on your face," this lady cried, patting her son's hand fondly. "Freddy is to escort you and I am to go as your chaperone. How exciting! I have always longed to see the inside of the Lanston house. They say the ballroom is—" she rattled on in this manner while Thalia looked desperately at her mother as if to assure herself this was not the truth, but she merely received the usual tight-lipped smile and nod which her mother reserved for those moments when she was feeling particularly generous.

Thalia could not enter into the remainder of the conversation, staring instead with dismay at the tips of her yellow slippers, which were peeking out from beneath the hem of her crinoline, a fact which was also noticed by Freddy, who gazed upon them lasciviously when his mother was not demanding his clever opinions upon various topics. Thalia did not even hear her sister's feeble efforts at the piano and had to be almost dragged to the instrument herself, she was in such a daze, performing so poorly that Mrs. Cornfield began to wonder if this girl would indeed be a good enough match for her precious son. Thalia was made even more miserable by the realization that her mother was growing increasingly irritated by what she considered to be her daughter's deliberate rudeness and rebellious refusal to play correctly.

Flora, however, acquitted herself well, having at last given up her unavailing efforts upon Thomas Cornfield and hanging instead upon Frederic's every word as he recounted an adventure in which he had stopped a runaway horse on Regent Street at great risk to his own life and welfare.

At last the tedious evening was at an end. Mrs. Horrocks arose primly and said that she liked her daughters to go to bed early.

"Of course," shrieked Mrs. Cornfield, with a nervous giggle, "for their beauty sleep. They are such charming girls." She hugged Flora who was closest to her and then came over to overwhelm Thalia in her capacious embrace.

Her husband, who was almost asleep upon the other sofa, blinked rapidly and, finally realizing that the party was at an end, rose to his feet, declaring repeatedly that they must see each other again soon as it was always so interesting to talk to good friends.

Freddy, under the pretence of shaking Thalia's hand as a farewell, whispered to her, "I shall dream of you tonight. I always think of you as I am going to sleep." Thalia knew well what sort of thoughts these must be as he lay upstairs in his own room. She shuddered to think that he could toy with her in his thoughts without her consent.

As they exited, Mrs. Cornfield called out in her brassy voice, "Don't forget, Thalia dear, about the ball. We shall be seeing you for that in a few days," and then they were down the steps and into the carriage again for the brief ride home.

But the ordeal was not yet over, as both Thalia's mother and her stepfather berated her soundly for her lack of manners.

"You did not even thank Mrs. Cornfield for her kind offer to escort you," Mrs. Horrocks declared. "If she had not done so, I probably would not have permitted you to go.

Mr. Horrocks followed up this attack with a comment upon her piano-playing efforts, demanding to know how she could perform so creditably for him in the evenings and fail so completely before the Cornfields.

"I think she must be reminded that you have not raised your daughters to behave in such a manner," he said to Mrs. Horrocks as they stepped out of the carriage before their own home. "She is not to go out on calls or receive any until the night of the ball, and then we will see whether her conduct has improved."

Thalia thought wildly for a moment that if she behaved poorly enough they would not permit her to go with Frederic and his mother, but then decided that this benefit would not outweigh her loss if she was unable to attend the first and probably the last Society Ball to which she would ever be invited.

She followed them meekly into the house saying, "Yes, Mama. Yes, Mr. Horrocks," at inappropriate moments, as she was not listening at all to their reproaches and gratefully escaped up the stairs into her own room, where she sat by the light of a candle, reading the pages of her manuscript and consoling herself with this, her ticket to escape.

Chapter Seven

*The Ball Given by the Viscountess Lanston at Which Thalia
Is Beguiled by the Handsome Marquis of Parringdon and
Mr. Lanston Introduces Miss Stillwater to Polite Society*

MRS. HORROCKS KEPT FIRMLY to her decision to punish her
errant daughter by confining her to the house, except upon one
day early in the week, when they went upon an expedition to the
mercer's to choose material for Thalia's ball dress.

Mrs. Horrocks was a staunch advocate of bright colours and
shiny material; she was drawn immediately to the section of silks
and satins and commanded the elderly, bespectacled shopkeeper
to pull down bolt after bolt of the material, which she fingered
suspiciously. At last she chose a brilliant magenta satin, which
seemed to her the appropriate hue for her daughter's vivid
colouring. Thalia, however, had been drawn to the section of
organdies, fine muslins printed with soft floral patterns, and she
begged her mother to consider one of these as the fabric for the underskirt of the proposed dress. Mrs. Horrocks disliked discussing
such matters with her daughter before a shopkeeper, especially as
he agreed delightedly with the young lady that organdy was so
suitable for the young. Hoping to avoid an unpleasant scene, she
generously allowed Thalia to choose a pale organdy imprinted

with pink flowers, and then swept her and the bolts of material out of the shop and into the carriage for the drive to her dressmaker.

The dressmaker, Mrs. Meeker, was a pale, thin-lipped woman who got along well with Mrs. Horrocks, as they always agreed on what was fashionable. Mrs. Meeker smiled and stroked the magenta satin with her stiff, work-coarsened fingers, but turned up her nose and sniffed at the sight of the organdy. However, the two materials did match well and the dressmaker finally reluctantly agreed to use the organdy as the underskirt. She demonstrated to Mrs. Horrocks, her fingers making quick, fluttering gestures in the air about Thalia, how she would design the dress, looping the satin up on either side and gathering it at the back in a small bustle.

"It is all the mode just now," she said primly, and Mrs. Horrocks eagerly agreed that this was just the sort of dress which Thalia required.

They left with the promise that the garment would be done within two days, and continued on in a relentless search for the necessary accessories. Mrs. Horrocks chose these while Thalia stood by helplessly: long gloves dyed to a brilliant pink, soft kid dancing slippers also coloured to the same hue, a shiny new cloak of a salmon shade which clashed with the other colours, and a pink taffeta sash, for if Mrs. Horrocks had any reservations about her dressmaker it was that Mrs. Meeker often left the dresses too plain. The last stop was a milliner's at which Mrs. Horrocks left a shred of the satiny material with the instructions that several ostrich plumes were to be dyed to match it

Upon their return home Thalia discovered that her mother had taken a very unprecedented step—she had engaged a dancing master. He was an elderly gentleman with greying hair and rather stiff joints who was to instruct both Thalia and her sister in the fine art of dancing for an hour each day. He began by explaining the figures of the various square dances they would be called upon to perform at a ball: the old Sir Roger de Coverley, the quadrille, and the contredanse.

Thalia was a lovely dancer, instinctively graceful, always in time to the music which the dancing master provided by humming tunelessly while tapping his cane upon the floor to keep time.

Flora, however, was awkward and absolutely incapable of under-standing the principle of rhythm. By sheer diligence, she eventually memorized the various figures which Thalia could guess at unerringly and, well pleased, the dancing master promised them a new dance.

Unfortunately when he arrived for their lessons the next day and began to twirl Thalia about the room in "a waltz," Flora recalled the scandal attached to this word and went off looking for her mother. Thalia found the waltz enchanting; the lively motion made her feel not quite herself, more vivacious, more yielding. As the dancing master led her gracefully into a breath-taking turn, Mrs. Horrocks appeared on the threshold, Flora's head visible behind her shoulder. She clapped her hands together sharply, claiming their attention and then said fiercely, "Mr. Brown, I had no notion that you would take it upon yourself to teach my daughters," she drew Flora close to her, "such an immoral dance as the waltz." Her voice lowered instinctively at that offensive word. "You are dismissed."

Much bewildered, the old gentleman took up his hat and cane and, bowing politely, scurried down the hallway and out the door.

Thalia was downcast, for she had looked to the dancing lessons as the bright spots in her tedious days, but she considered that she was ready for the ball and did not complain about the abrupt halt to her lesson. Instead, she took herself off to her bed-room to engage in what had become her daily penmanship exercises.

She was now almost to the close of her Novel, relating rapidly various adventures which befell Mariana in the course of obtaining her livelihood, not the least of which was a chapter in which she was kidnapped by the odious Baron Crofton and only saved by the earnest endeavours of her young Protector. Thalia had determined that the Novel should end with a great reconciliation scene in which the daughter would discover her true mother, now respectably wed. But she had yet to write this scene as there were still many details to be worked out.

As the day of the ball grew near and Thalia felt more and more oppressed and listless, she began to importune her mother to allow her to ride in the Park in order to get a little fresh air and exercise. Noting that Thalia's complexion was becoming very pale and unhealthy, Mrs. Horrocks at last gave her consent on the day of the ball itself, if Thalia was accompanied by both Miss Mallet and Flora.

Thus the three rode out early in the afternoon on a very grey and damp day. Flora was an inexpert rider, as she was frightened of horses, and they made their way slowly through the crowded and muddy streets to the Park. As they were proceeding down Oxford Street, Thalia saw again the shabby bear and his master. Upon such a gloomy day, the bear seemed almost human, unable to lumber about in his usual cheerful manner but merely shuffling his feet a little and making pathetic begging gestures with his paws. Thalia felt oppressed by this sight and turned away in disgust, but Miss Mallet and Flora were delighted. They devoted several minutes to watching this spectacle and did not continue on their way until the bear had dropped to all four feet, seemingly disgruntled by the boredom of his existence.

The Park was nearly empty upon such an overcast day; they passed few other riders although there were many barouches and landaus passing down Rotten Row, bearing their lovely female occupants. Thalia suddenly heard a gasp from Miss Mallet beside her, and looking in the direction pointed out by Miss Mallet's quivering finger, she espied Susannah and Lynton in one of these carriages, a small golden barouche drawn by a superbly matched chestnut pair.

Susannah was wearing the pale orange dress in which Thalia had first seen her; upon her lap was a huge, placid, orange-and-white striped cat who looked about with disdainful golden eyes. Susannah's eyes however were not disdainful; she was gazing upon Lynton with unconcealed fondness while he nibbled shamelessly upon her neck. Thalia tried to get their attention by waving her hands about wildly and bouncing up and down on her mount, but Miss Mallet, taking command in an unprecedented way, led Thalia and Flora quickly out of the Park, declaring that they must return home immediately.

"Do you know what type of woman that was?" the governess asked, all ashudder, as they left Rotten Row. "I know it was your cousin but the female with him—Miss Thalia, you must remember that one must, under no circumstances, even look at one of these—" Miss Mallet stopped, unable to think of a suitable word. Thalia was crushed by these circumstances but took comfort in the thought that tonight her temporary bondage would be ended, at least for a little while.

However as they passed down Oxford Street a very unfortunate incident occurred. Thalia was watching her horse pick his way carefully about the heaps of refuse in the street when she heard an oddly familiar voice saying with great pleasure, "Why, Miss Thalia Lawrence. I have been searching for you this fortnight. Where have you disappeared to?"

Looking up quickly, Thalia saw the slender, elegant form of the Marquis of Parringdon astride an enormous and beautiful black horse. For a moment, dressed as he was in a slim, well-fitting black coat and a dark hat, she almost mistook him for the dark hero of her dreams, except for his blond curls beneath the hat brim, his languid moustache, and the warm look in his blue eyes.

Flora and Miss Mallet had halted behind her and were staring aghast at the impertinent young man.

"Sir, I fear you are mistaken," Thalia replied in a clear but trembling voice, and pressed her horse forward. She could not however deny herself a backward glance, and saw that he had stopped amidst the swirling traffic and was staring after her sadly, and with a puzzled look when he saw Miss Mallet and Flora draw their horses abreast of hers.

"Shocking! Shocking!" declared Miss Mallet in horrified tones. "What is the world coming to when a gentleman accosts a girl he does not know on the street in that manner?"

"But he called her Thalia," Flora pointed out, with a sly sideways glance at her sister.

"He called me Thalia Lawrence," Thalia replied in troubled tones. "Obviously he was mistaken."

"But there are not many girls named Thalia in all of London—or England for that matter," Flora continued obstinately. "I have never heard of one."

Thalia did not wish to discuss the matter further and cast a withering glance at her sister, who lapsed into silence.

Miss Mallet however was not through with this episode. "First, it was incorrect for him to speak to you at all," she said reflectively, "for you had not recognized him and the lady must always initiate the conversation. You did not, did you, Thalia?"

"No," replied the girl sharply. "You saw that I was looking downwards. I did not know he—anyone was there until he spoke."

"And then," went on Miss Mallet, satisfied upon this point, "you should have given him the cut direct, my dear, or at least avoided his glance, rather than replying in that bold manner. It was quite improper."

"I only wished to inform him that he was mistaken," Thalia replied with some irritation. "If I had not answered, he might have continued to believe I was the girl he sought and tried to pursue me."

Miss Mallet glanced back nervously to assure herself that he was not doing this, as in fact he was, but a huge van of goods cut him off from her sight, and she turned around, relieved.

As soon as they had arrived at Russell Square and dismounted from their horses, Flora ran into the house, almost knocking aside the elderly Joseph in the process, and Thalia could hear her shrill voice recounting their various adventures to Mrs. Horrocks through the sitting-room window. Within a few moments, she was summoned there, and for a time it seemed as if her attendance at the ball was in jeopardy. At length Mrs. Horrocks relented, as she felt this was the last social event Thalia would attend before her engagement to Mr. Cornfield was announced, for she and Mrs. Cornfield had decided that Frederic should propose to Thalia that night.

"So romantic, at a ball, the flowers, the candles, the music," Mrs. Cornfield had sighed. "That is how George asked for my hand." Mrs. Horrocks disapproved of the practice of young men announcing their intentions to the young woman before asking her parents, but she was willing to go along with Mrs. Cornfield's scheme, as Freddy's mother had promised her that he would come to call upon Mr. Horrocks the very next morning. Therefore, she sent Thalia upstairs to put on the dress which had just been delivered that afternoon and bustled off to see that the plans for dinner were going smoothly.

As Thalia dressed she found herself thinking about her cousin Letty, who had sent several urgent notes begging Thalia to call upon her. Mrs. Horrocks had insisted that Thalia return all of these with various polite refusals. Letty had finally come herself, arriving one morning very distraught, and impolite and commanding as never before. But as Mrs. Horrocks insisted that Thalia had only five minutes to spare from her busy schedule and as she sat in the drawing room with the two girls, Letty was not able to take advantage of this opportunity to confide in her cousin.

Letty was facing the prospect of the ball with resignation, knowing that her mother thought of it as her last chance to attract a wealthy husband for her daughter, as well as providing an excellent diversion to take Letty's mind off her unfortunate tendre for her younger brother's tutor, who had been abruptly dismissed. The Viscountess had obeyed her husband's command not to mention the matter to the girl, but she watched her daughter constantly and sorrowfully, ready to relieve the pangs of first love which she felt sure Letty must be suffering. However Letty showed no signs of sadness, although of late she displayed an increasing tendency to do as she wished, refusing all of the cheerfully coloured and elaborate ball dresses which her mother proposed and choosing instead a simple white dress, trimmed only with roses, which made her look almost as if she were a bride.

As the day approached, she did not manifest any of the signs of nervousness and timidity which usually overcame her before large social events, and the Viscountess began to think her scheme would work and Letty would indeed find her future husband upon this night. She thought it odd that previously no man had offered for her, for while there was a large surplus of marriageable girls in London, Letty was an heiress of a well-known and wealthy family and of passable good looks. She could only assume that her daughter was unable to flirt and converse wittily and took many opportunities to school Letty in these necessary qualities.

Her efforts seemed to have been successful, for as Letty greeted her guests at the front door, she was calm and charming, remarking prettily on the ladies' dresses and fluttering her eyes provocatively at the gentlemen.

Thalia surrounded by the two Cornfields was among the first to arrive, attired in the dazzling new pink cloak with equally shocking pink plumes waving from her hair. Letty could merely murmur a conventional hello, as Mrs. Cornfield was close behind Thalia, effusing to the Viscountess upon the too, too charming decor and her equally charming daughter Letitia.

As soon as they had passed through the gauntlet of the receiving line, Thalia excused herself and rushed off to the dressing room with Mrs. Cornfield in close pursuit. At the moment this room, ordinarily the bedroom of one of Letty's younger sisters, was empty, although later it would be packed from wall to wall with young misses and ladies primping before the mirrors.

"It is utterly divine," shrieked Mrs. Cornfield, standing in the midst of the room and turning about, taking in the shining marble-topped washstands and the glittering gold-framed mirrors. "But the paper is a trifle subdued," she said, frowning at the walls which were covered with a delicate floral print. "Don't you agree, Thalia dear?"

"A bit," said Thalia, who staunchly disagreed with Mrs. Cornfield's opinions. "You will find a much prettier paper in Letty's room, next door. You must slip in there and look at it. No one will be about, I assure you."

"Oh, if I may," simpered Mrs. Cornfield, avid to explore the entire house from top to bottom. As soon as she had sneaked dramatically out of the door, Thalia removed her cloak and set about altering her dress as she had planned. For this purpose she had brought with her a small pair of silver shears and she began to cut off the tiny stitches which attached the hideous pink overskirt to the rest of the dress. This was difficult, especially in the back, and Thalia was rather careless, slashing into the satiny material in her haste to remove it before Mrs. Cornfield reappeared.

Fortunately this lady had not been content to look merely at Letty's room but was tiptoeing down the corridor opening all of the doors and observing every detail of the furnishings with great delight. By the time she had completed her tour, Thalia had retied the pink sash about her waist to hide her clumsy alterations, hidden the remnants of the overskirt in a cupboard, and sabotaged the pink plumes.

"Oh dear!" cried Mrs. Cornfield, re-entering and seeing Thalia holding the now-bedraggled feathers. "What has happened to our lovely plumes?"

"I was trying to readjust them," Thalia said calmly, "and they slipped from my hand and into this pitcher of water. It is very unfortunate, is it not? But I suppose I will have to do without them."

She quickly thrust them into the same empty cupboard where she had hidden the pink material.

"And your dress—" said Mrs. Cornfield, puzzled. "1 remember your mama telling me that it had a most attractive overskirt and bustle. But it is so plain and simple, not at all what one should wear to such a fashionable event."

She herself was attired in a blazing orange dress covered with ruching and frills and rows of multi-coloured cameo buttons.

"At the last moment the dressmaker decided to omit the overskirt," Thalia said, turning to a mirror to readjust her hair. She had chosen some pink roses from one of the many vases in the room and was pinning them in among the dark curls piled high on her head. "I prefer the dress this way myself."

Mrs. Cornfield frowned, as she now thought her future daughter-in-law looked much too inconspicuous in her simple, flower-sprigged muslin gown, ornamented only with the heavy ruffle at the bottom, the wide pink taffeta sash and the rich lace upon the low neckline. And wearing only flowers in her hair, much too missish, thought Mrs. Cornfield, who had envied her those brilliant plumes. She herself wore a tiara of coral, heedless of the fact that it clashed with the orange of her dress.

Thalia, however, smiled at her reflection in the mirror, well content with the simplicity of the dress and style, for it highlighted her delicate features and rich colouring, both of which had been overshadowed by the dazzling magenta.

After several minutes in which Mrs. Cornfield fussed with her fading blond hair, which was already beginning to escape in little wisps from its pins, and applied a little powder surreptitiously to her florid complexion, they again descended the stairs to the ballroom, ablaze with candles and now partially filled.

As they crossed the shining parquet floor to where Frederic sat upon a small gilt chair, looking very uncomfortable in his black cutaway and top hat, Mrs. Cornfield pressed into Thalia's hand a cologne-drenched handkerchief, saying, "Nibble upon this during the evening; it will make your eyes sparkle." As the cologne contained a high percentage of alcohol it would indeed have had this effect, but Thalia needed no such artificial stimulus. Her eyes glowed with excitement, appearing almost too large for her small, finely boned face, as she looked about at the elegantly dressed ladies and gentlemen milling about the room. Even the presence of Freddy and his mother could not dampen her high spirits.

Mrs. Cornfield was not to be daunted by the fact that she knew none of those present, and led Thalia and Freddy about the room, swooping down upon groups of people, boldly introducing herself, her son, and his future wife, at which words Thalia always cringed and looked about desperately for someone to contradict this information. There were many handsome and titled young men among the guests who looked at Thalia approvingly until they heard Mrs. Cornfield's speech, whereupon they turned away to talk to their friends. Mrs. Cornfield's presence had a peculiar effect upon the people she spoke to. They murmured the coolest and politest pleasantries, then simply turned about or moved off, until there was finally no one who would speak to the little party. They stood against one wall, listening to the laughter and conversation of those about them, totally ignored. Thalia considered that if her mother had contrived to have her attend a ball and yet prevent her from meeting any one of the aristocracy, she had certainly chosen well in picking Mrs. Cornfield as her chaperone.

The orchestra, which had been tuning up for some minutes, launched into their first number, and Freddy, as Thalia's escort, claimed the privilege of the first dance. Mrs. Cornfield smiled benevolently as he led her to the floor. He was, as Thalia had expected, a dreadful dancer, unable to remember even the simplest figures of the dance and leaving damp spots upon her dress every time he clasped her about the waist for a turn. There were few people dancing and Thalia felt herself blush with mortification at the thought that all of those watching would remember her as the girl with the awkward partner. She tried to perform gracefully in those moments when she was alone or paired with another partner, desperately afraid that no one else would ask for a dance and she would be forced to dance with Freddy all evening. Letty was leading the dance with her father, and as she passed Thalia in one of the figures, she whispered quickly, "Thalia, I must speak to you alone in the study in ten minutes."

Letty danced the next two dances with two of the handsomest young men present, laughing and chatting with them in a flirtatious manner, while Thalia sat watching glumly on the side lines. She looked about for Lynton, who would be the only other male present who she knew, but he was nowhere in sight; Thalia reflected that his parents would be outraged at his absence from his sister's ball. She thought perhaps that he was with Susannah—they had certainly appeared very much in love—and wondered how this would affect Susannah's occupation. From her own experience writing about her Heroine she had discovered that Love was a very unprofitable emotion for a young girl engaged in Susannah's business; it meant that she would have to turn down wealthier customers in order to find a few moments of time to spend with her True Love.

At length the dances were finished and as the orchestra started another number, Thalia saw that Letty was excusing herself from yet another fashionable gentleman and slipping out of the room. Thalia had already decided how she could escape from Mrs. Cornfield's ministrations; she pointed out to her some people she had not yet approached and, as Mrs. Cornfield hurried in their direction, Thalia dashed the other way, ploughing through several groups of people in her efforts to cover her escape.

She found the study quickly and stepped inside, shutting the heavy door behind her. Letty stood before the mantel; she looked young and beautiful in the white dress with roses as ornaments in her brown hair, but her eyes were unnaturally dark and her complexion unusually pale. She seemed agitated and restless; she paced about the room as Thalia sank into the comfortable chair behind the desk.

"Thalia," she said in a strange voice. "I have something to tell you which you must tell to no one else. I must confide in one person in the event something goes wrong and you are the only one I can trust. Thalia, I am going to elope!"

Thalia looked at her wide-eyed. "Who—when?" she gasped.

"You have heard me mention Mr. Crofts, the tutor—I should say . . . former tutor—of my younger brother," Letty said, resuming her pacing. "We have fallen in love. We kept our feelings secret for many months, for you know my parents would not allow me to marry someone of his social status. As it has turned out, Edward," she blushed, and added, "(that is Mr. Crofts's given name) recently inherited a small sum of money and a house in Brighton from his uncle and thought we could be married. So he asked my father for his permission and of course was refused. Thalia," she said desperately," I could not let him go. You may not understand it perhaps, but I feel that I have changed greatly in the last fortnight. I am no longer going to allow my parents to decide what is best for me for in this matter; they do not know what that is. I am sure they will soon be reconciled to the idea, but for now that is of no consequence, for it is only Edward's approval that I require. In any event, Edward and I have made plans to elope. He has been writing to me at Lady Guenevere's house and he has prepared his house for my arrival this Sunday. We will be married as soon as I arrive in Brighton; he has a Special License and the banns have already been read. I wanted you to know, for although I am going to write to my parents as soon as we are married, I am not going to tell them my whereabouts for I am sure my father would plan something desperate. But in case," her voice faltered, "in case anything should happen to one of my sisters—or my father—or mother—I want you to write me immediately." Thalia, who had been dumbfounded by this entire revelation, nodded dazedly and dutifully memorized the address which Letty pressed upon her.

"Your Lady Guenevere has been so helpful to me," Letty murmured. "I have visited her often to pick up Edward's letters. At first she was angry and quizzed me as my parents would have, but she at last decided that Edward and I seem admirably well suited and she consented to aid us. Tomorrow she is going to send an invitation that I have written, supposedly from my Aunt Catherine in Hampstead, to come and spend a few days with her. My aunt is fortunately out of town, and when the coachman sets me down at her estate, Lady Guenevere will be waiting nearby in her carriage and drive me to the station where I will take the train to Brighton. Thalia, I am so happy! It is so good to be surrounded by so many dear friends, as you and Lady Guenevere, and to know that I will soon be Edward's wife. We are going to start a small academy for boys, you know," she added blithely.

There were footsteps in the hall outside and Letty glanced about sharply. "Of course, we must go back," she said quickly. "We will be missed and I have already promised these dances. My partners will be searching for me. But, Thalia, I want to write to you also. As I know your mother reads everything you receive, I am going to send you a letter in care of Lady Guenevere. You must go there on the following Monday; she will know if our plan has succeeded."

They quitted the study abruptly, and as they were hurrying back to the ballroom, Thalia said shyly, "Letty, I wish you the greatest happiness in the future." Letty smiled upon her fondly and then rushed forward to greet her waiting partner. Thalia thought a little enviously that if Letty was not really interested in these handsome young men that she should point a few of them in her cousin's direction.

Mrs. Cornfield had been looking anxiously for her charge, and now, spotting her through the crowds, bore down upon her like a battleship with Freddy in tow. Shouting loudly, "Thalia, my dear, Freddy has been searching for you everywhere," she pushed them together and out onto the dance floor.

There were many dancers now and Thalia felt less conspicuous with her awkward partner. At one point, he stepped upon her skirt, and almost tore the flounce from the rest of the dress. Instinctively Thalia snapped at him. As Letty was floating by at this moment, she noticed Thalia's distress and, smiling at her cousin, whispered sweetly, "Everything will be all right, Thalia." Thalia did not perceive what Letty could have meant and spent the remainder of the dance concentrating upon avoiding Freddy's heavy feet.

When the dance had ended and the pair had rejoined Mrs. Cornfield, who had struck up a conversation with a very uncomfortable-looking military man, Thalia soon saw her cousin's meaning. The handsome gentleman with whom Letty had been dancing was making his way through the crowd to Thalia's place and begged her for the pleasure of the next dance. Thalia felt a little pang of annoyance, for she would have preferred to find her own partners rather than receive Letty's cast-offs. However, she found him an admirable dancer and enjoyed immensely her few minutes on the floor. The young man seemed charmed with her also, complimenting her upon her dancing skill and her appearance, until he returned her to Mrs. Cornfield, who pointedly introduced Freddy as Thalia's fiancé. However this partner's subsequent desertion was no problem, as she soon had a stream of others, all pointed her way by Letty, but all seeming to enjoy Thalia's company. The only unpleasantness occurred when the following dance was a waltz, for Mrs. Cornfield, under instructtions from Mrs. Horrocks, enjoyed berating the young men for asking her charge to dance such an immoral dance. Thalia watched regretfully during the waltzes and polkas (which had also been forbidden to her) while Letty whirled about the room, obviously enjoying herself.

The time passed in this way for quite a while. It was nearing the time for supper when Thalia, passing through the figures of a complicated dance with a new partner, saw with a little shock of horror that Letty was dancing with Lord Parringdon. He was a superb dancer and they were undoubtedly the most striking couple on the floor; Thalia could hear the buzz of conversation as the dowagers present speculated upon this handsome pair. Thalia realized with a sinking feeling that Letty could have met the young man again at Lady Guenevere's house and wondered if they had cleared up the matter of her status. The Marquis seemed entranced by Letty and by some clever remark which she was undoubtedly making. He did not even notice the other dancers on the floor and Thalia felt an unexpectedly sharp pang of envy.

She was horrified when at the start of the next dance she saw the Marquis coming her way, stopping politely to bow to several attractive young ladies. Letty had, Thalia thought angrily, sent him her way as she had all her other partners. The dance was a waltz, and as soon as the Marquis reached them, Mrs. Cornfield began her usual tirade. However, he was not at all intimidated as the others had been; he seemed amused and said in a cool voice, "Ridiculous," sweeping Thalia from Mrs. Cornfield's side and out onto the dance floor.

For a few moments, Thalia had to concentrate on her steps, for she had only danced a few measures of a waltz before, but she soon found it easy, for the Marquis was an excellent partner, moving her around the room with a firm and confident grasp.

"Miss Lawrence, we meet again," he murmured into her ear, "and under very strange circumstances. I had not thought to find you here. And in such an absurdly innocent, although I admit, charming, dress. And your supposed chaperone—a remarkable woman. You are certainly an enterprising young woman."

Thalia first blushed, then grew angry as she realized he still thought her one of the pretty horsebreakers. But his misapprehension, she slowly decided, would give her the chance to indulge in a harmless flirtation.

"Sir," she said, looking up provocatively, "I understand that you have been searching for me."

"Then we did meet on Oxford Street," he said musingly. "And you cut me so cruelly," he added in a mock-sorrowful tone. "I would not have thought you could be so unkind."

"Indeed, sir, it was your fault," Thalia replied, her eyes conveying a message which contradicted her words, "for you know I ought to have recognized you first."

"How could I have waited?" he asked in pleading tones, although with an amused smile. "For you were keeping your beautiful dark eyes fixed upon the ground; in truth I was on my way to the Park in the hopes that I would find you there. And what have you been doing during my days of loneliness and gloom when just one glance from your eyes would have filled my heart with life again?"

Thalia almost giggled at this dramatic question. "I have been very busy," she answered suggestively. "You understand." She fluttered her dark lashes a bit.

"Cruel Beauty," the Marquis returned, "when I might be a good friend to you." His tightened grasp upon her waist conveyed what type of friend he wished to be.

Thalia, remembering their previous encounter and feeling dizzy as a result of his closeness, felt incapable of a response. She abandoned herself instead to the sensuous appeal of the dance, content to respond instinctively to his lead as he turned her about. Just as the dance was about to end, he abruptly deviated from the usual circular path taken by the dancers about the room, and waltzed her into the conservatory, where he sat her down upon a bench among the flowers. It was dim among the ferns and fuchsias and the room was entirely empty. Thalia felt suddenly afraid in the sweet-smelling darkness with the Marquis standing before her, gazing down upon her.

"You are lovely," he murmured slowly.

"You are a very good dancer, sir," she responded calmly, trying to mask her apprehension.

"But not your equal," he said, seating himself upon the bench and passing his arm about her waist. "Where have you been hiding yourself? Have you just arrived in London from some sleepy village?"

Thalia trembled a little at his touch but answered coolly, "Yes, I have just come up from Brighton, where I was born and raised." She delighted in inventing tales and had soon given him an entire history of her upbringing as the youngest daughter of a Brighton merchant. As she knew little of such a life, the Marquis soon perceived that she was not telling the truth, but he continued to ply her with questions about this fiction, amused by her innocently absurd answers.

They had been talking for some time when Thalia suddenly said, "Oh! But I must return to Mrs. Cornfield, you know, my chaperone—she will be looking for me."

"Of course, she will not be," the Marquis replied cynically. "A charming fabrication this—chaperone, as you call her. But quite unnecessary with me. I am taking you up to supper."

Thalia, feeling as if she were in a dream, assented to this plan breathlessly and taking her arm firmly in his own, Stacey led her back through the ballroom. He was easily one of the most handsome men present, and the ladies whispered behind their fans as he and Thalia walked by. Fortunately Thalia could see no sign of Freddy and his mother, for they were conducting a room-by-room search of the house for her, and she went up to supper with the Marquis, becoming a little intoxicated by the champagne and nibbling upon the excellent dishes. She found that champagne loosened her tongue and was soon flirting outrageously with the Marquis, recounting various incidents of her childhood and even telling him of the sad bear on Oxford Street.

"He reminds me of myself," she said, a little downcast. The Marquis looked at her with concern. He had recognized that she was slowly beginning to tell him the truth; he gathered that she had been sadly oppressed in her childhood by a bullying mama.

"Sir," said Thalia, brightening and turning to him with her most engaging smile. "If you wish to win my favours, you must free that bear." She was confident that he could not do this, but wondered for a little moment what gift he would expect her to make in return. She blushed at the visions which rose unbidden to her mind. The Marquis added to her confusion by smiling at her meaningfully and taking her hand into his own, kissing it gently.

At this moment Frederic Cornfield, his round face red with anger, burst into the supper room, followed by his mama.

"Unhand that girl, you Snake," Freddy shouted dramatically, laying hold of the Marquis' elegant black jacket and trying to pull him from his seat. "She is Mine—my fiancée —my future wife. You have toyed with her under my very nose. I will kill you, sir."

He actually looked as if he was ready to strike the Marquis. Thalia rose to try to prevent this. Mrs. Cornfield shrieked, "Oh, Freddy, be careful!"

Freddy, screwing up his countenance and waving his fist about in the air, lunged at the Marquis, who calmly stepped aside, and Freddy fell across the table, splattering himself with gravy and breaking several plates and glasses. The other guests were all moving from their seats, horrified. Freddy was unmoved by his ridiculous appearance and first failure. He threw himself at the Marquis again, this time receiving in return a well-placed blow on the chin, which sent him reeling back against the chairs. Mrs. Cornfield was jumping up and down, screaming in her high, shrill voice. Thalia tried vainly to capture one of Freddy's arms and hold him back as he struggled forward for his third attempt.

At that moment, Lynton appeared in the doorway, brought upstairs by the sounds of the screams which were drifting down to the ballroom. He immediately laid hold of the dazed, but still fighting, Freddy, and with the Marquis holding his other arm, forcibly removed him from the room. His mother, distraught over the manner in which her son had been treated, followed, wailing aloud, and Thalia was left alone among the broken glass and crockery, feeling completely foolish. With relief she saw Susannah at the door, and without wondering why Susannah was at such a gathering, ran into her arms, weeping hysterically. Susannah gently led her to a deserted bedroom on the third floor and spoke to her softly until Thalia felt calmer.

Thalia was eventually coaxed into telling her story to Susannah, and as Miss Stillwater went into gales of laughter over the conduct of Mrs. Cornfield and her son and over Thalia's flirtation with the Marquis, Thalia soon saw the humorous side of the situation and began to laugh along with her. For a few minutes they giggled without pause, until Thalia stopped abruptly and asked hesitantly, "Susannah, how did you come to be here?"

"It's your cousin, Lynton," said Susannah, shaking her head fondly. "He insisted that I come. I told him I would not be welcome here, but he arrived at my door and demanded that I go off with him, without telling me where. And then he brought me here, knowing that I have always longed to go to such a party. And I could not understand why he wanted me to wear my best dress." She smiled placidly and gazed down at her lovely cream-coloured satin gown.

"You look beautiful, Susannah," Thalia replied, taking in her elegant coiffure of cascading golden curls and the breathtakingly simple gown. "No one will realize that you do not belong."

"Only wait and you will see," answered Susannah with a rueful smile. "But Lynton must be wondering what has happened to me. Shall we go down?"

They encountered Lynton at the bottom of the grand stairs. He watched Susannah adoringly as she approached him and kissed her hand affectionately before he turned to Thalia and said, "They are repairing the young man in one of the drawing rooms. It seems he cut his hand on some of the glass. Who is he, Thalia? Why was he fighting over you?"

"That is Mr. Frederic Cornfield," Thalia replied acidly. "You remember I told you of him that day in the Park."

Lynton lifted his eyebrows and nodded with understanding.

"Poor Thalia," he said, patting her upon the head like a child. "We must find someone else for you immediately. Come with Susannah and me into the ballroom; he will not be bothering you for a while."

Thalia knew the impropriety of her actions but could not resist a chance to savour the last few minutes left to her at this ball.

As they entered the room, Thalia a few paces behind Susannah and Lynton, there was a rapid buzz of conversation. Thalia thought at first that everyone was discussing the fight in the supper room, but soon realized that all eyes were upon Susannah, whom Lynton was leading from group to group, introducing as Miss Stillwater. There was a curious reaction to her presence. The ladies looked suspicious and unpleasant, as many of them had coveted Lynton as a husband for themselves or their daughters, but the men reacted even more strangely. They became red-faced, hemmed and hawed, looked aside, greeted Susannah too familiarly or contemplated her handsome figure lecherously.

Gradually the truth about Susannah became known to the ladies. Several of them scurried about the ballroom, whispering furiously to others behind their fans, and as Lynton moved on with his companion, they began to cut her, turning aside when he tried to introduce her and moving off icily to other parts of the room. Thalia followed behind, a reluctant but curious eavesdropper, hearing little snatches of the conversation they left in their wake.

"A charming girl," one gentleman was saying, whereupon one of the ladies of his party said coldly, "What can she be thinking of, trying to foist herself upon Polite Society in this manner? The poor Viscountess, I shudder to think of what she is going through."

Another well-dressed young swell whistled beneath his breath, saying, "Lynton Lanston is indeed a lucky man. She is one of the warmest and most intelligent Cyprians in the city," while the lady at his side remarked, "What a shocking display of vulgarity! She should be sent out immediately!"

Nearly all conversation in the room had stopped as Lynton approached his parents, with Susannah, her cheeks flaming but her head held high, at his side.

"Mother, I wish to present to you, Miss Susannah Stillwater," Lynton said boldy. The Viscountess stared at Susannah through her lorgnette before pointedly looking away from her and saying to her son, "Lynton, I beg you to leave this moment."

The Viscount, however, although a little ill at ease, was determined to be pleasant. He approved of his son's choice of a companion for the lighter moments, and though he thought the boy should have known better than to bring the young woman to this event, he considered it rather a good joke.

"May I have the pleasure of this dance, Miss Stillwater?" he asked elegantly, for although the orchestra was still playing, there was no one upon the floor.

"It would be my pleasure, sir," replied Susannah, giving him a lovely curtsey and a grateful smile. They moved off onto the floor while the Viscountess begged someone nearby for some smelling salts. Letty had had been watching this scene from the opposite side of the room. As all eyes were upon the Viscount dancing with the improper young female, she crossed the floor quickly and took

Lynton's arm, dragging him out onto the dance floor. A few brave couples then joined them and when the dance had ended, Letty helped to put an end to the chilling atmosphere in the room by walking up to Susannah and saying distinctly, "Miss Stillwater, how fortunate we are to have you with us. It is a great pleasure to see you again."

Having won the approval of both the host and his innocent daughter, there was little the other ladies present could do but accept Susannah's company with good nature, although they all tried to avoid her gaze, staring at her only while she was dancing. Lynton soon found that it had been a mistake to bring Susannah with him, for she had no lack of partners but was constantly whirling about the floor with gentlemen of all ages. He stood by his mother for a while, but she, determined not to create a scene, had chosen to vent her hostility by not speaking to him, and he eventually went off in search of Thalia and begged her for a dance.

"I wonder where your Mr. Cornfield is?" he asked, turning her about the room to the strains of a waltz. He was not as good a partner as the Marquis, for he was very tense and held her stiffly as if she were a block of wood.

"I really should be looking for him," Thalia sighed, "perhaps after this dance. You know, Lynton, I am not allowed to dance a waltz."

"Are you not?" he remarked conversationally. "You are certainly doing that now. And very well, I might add."

"Oh, Lynton," Thalia replied, "it is my mother's rule. She would be—will be—most displeased with me. But I have had such a good time."

"I imagine you have," Lynton said, whirling her about so rapidly that she became giddy. "Were you dining with the Marquis of Parringdon? He's very charming, but a heartbreaker, I warn you, Cousin. He collects ladies' hearts as if they were trinkets."

"You know him?" Thalia asked timidly.

"A little," Lynton said. "He's quite a Man about Town. In all of the clubs, at all the races, in every gambling casino and night-house in London. Very irresponsible but very wealthy. He has a little opera dancer named Fifi or Arlette or some equally ridiculous

French name whom he has set up in a house in St. John's Wood. She is usually with him. I was surprised that she was not at Lady Guenevere's that evening."

The waltz ended, and Lynton, noting that Susannah had already been taken for the next dance and that his cousin appeared very much concerned, volunteered to escort her to the drawing room where she could rejoin her friends.

As Thalia was upset by the news she had just heard about the Marquis, she was at first absent-minded as Lynton propelled her out of the ballroom and into the front room. But as soon as she saw that it was Eustace Parringdon who was wrapping Frederic's injured finger with a handkerchief and plying him with brandy, she felt suddenly weak and sat down quickly upon a sofa. The Marquis, glancing up, gave her an amused smile, the kind which lifted the edges of his moustache, giving him a cynical appearance. Thalia became unexpectedly dizzy as if the champagne was just beginning to affect her.

Freddy was quite displeased at having this man whom he had tried to attack ministering to him. He kept muttering, "You shall pay for this, sir," or "My fiancée, you know," but had not even noticed Thalia's entrance. Mrs. Cornfield was also distressed and was hinting strongly to the Marquis that her son would recover faster if left to his own resources. The Marquis, taking no notice of her comments, was pressing brandy upon her also and as she imbibed this rapidly she became more and more belligerent

"My son is quite right," she said thickly, glaring at him with her prominent blue eyes. "A disgraceful act, when you knew my son, as the girl's escort, had the prerogative to take her up to supper. Young man, where did you learn your manners? I am sure you never had a mother like myself."

"Indeed, I did not," Stacey replied cheerfully. "I may in truth say that I have never had the—er—pleasure of meeting such a mother before tonight." As Mrs. Cornfield in her befuddled state could not tell if this were a jest or a compliment, she stared at him fishily over the rim of her glass.

"Stacey, I think you are wanted in the ballroom," said Lynton, observing this scene with great delight.

The Marquis shrugged his shoulders elegantly and, bowing politely to both Cornfields, came over to where Thalia sat and kissed her hand before quitting the room. This action almost prompted another fight, although by the time Frederic had struggled to his feet the marquis had strolled lazily from the room and he found that he was unable to stand without support. He began weaving about the room, muttering indistinctly, "The Snake! ... the Cur! . . . My fiancée!"

"I shall call for your carriage and then bring you to the door," Lynton offered politely, stepping from the room and leaving Thalia alone with the Cornfields. Mrs. Cornfield had become maudlin and was clinging to her son, crying and kissing his wrapped finger.

"My poor little Freddy," she wailed. "My brave, heroic son."

Thalia sat quietly with her hands folded in her lap, her mind filled with too many confusing emotions and thoughts for her to make any movement.

Within a few minutes, Lynton reappeared and dragged the drunken Frederic to the front door, supporting Mrs. Cornfield upon his other arm. Giving their coachman directions to stop in Russell Square first, he gave Thalia a rueful smile and closed the door upon the trio.

Crowded as they were into the small carriage, the Cornfields at last recognized Thalia's existence. Mrs. Cornfield could not quite decide whether the entire unfortunate episode had been Thalia's fault or whether she had been mesmerized by that "Evil Man" (as she referred to the Marquis). Therefore, she alternately glared at her and stroked her hand, saying sorrowfully, "Poor dear."

Thalia had hoped that the Cornfields would proceed immediately home after leaving her at her house, but Mrs. Cornfield insisted on coming in and telling the entire story to Thalia's mother. As her breath still smelt strongly of the brandy she had taken, Mrs. Horrocks decided to deal with the matter in the morning and escorted her friend firmly back to her carriage, instructing Thalia sharply to go up to her room and go to bed. While Thalia removed the ruined ball dress, she wondered what her Fate would be in the morning, for she knew she could not escape her mother's censure for the various crimes she had committed. But she was too fatigued to speculate upon this at length. She climbed into her bed to drift off into a sleep filled with dreams of the Marquis of Parringdon who was carrying her away into the fog.

Chapter Eight

*In Which Thalia's Plans for Freedom Are Discovered by
Her Mama and She Is Forced to Accept the Proposal of
Mr. Frederic Cornfield*

UNFORTUNATELY FOR THALIA, Mr. Frederic Cornfield did not
arrive the next morning to offer for her hand. As Mr. Horrocks had
remained home from the City in expectation of this visit, Thalia
was summoned to the study, and cross-examined upon her
conduct at the party by both of her parents. Thalia herself did not
have a clear understanding of all the past night's events, and she
was unable to invent one clear and logical account which would
absolve her of all blame. Barraged by her stepfather's gruff queries
and Mrs. Horrocks' sharp questions, she gave several conflicting
reports about the ball and finally was banished to her room until
such time as she confessed.

Mr. Horrocks stalked off to the bank, grumbling and swearing
about his stepdaughter's wilfulness; Mrs. Horrocks, her keys
clanking at her side like a jailer, accompanied Thalia upstairs and
conducted a minute search of the premises to be sure there were
no frivolous books with which Thalia could entertain herself
during her solitary confinement. She confiscated the Tennyson and
several volumes of light reading which she found hidden in the
bottom of the wardrobe, and then, to Thalia's horror, discovered

the Novel, in the lowest drawer of the writing desk. Recognizing her daughter's shockingly poor writing and realizing with chagrin that this was the reason for Thalia's dutiful application to penmanship exercises, Mrs. Horrocks also gathered up every pen, bottle of ink, and piece of paper in the room, leaving Thalia only a Bible with which to while away the hours.

Mrs. Horrocks was a singularly incurious woman; she never considered reading the contraband material; instead she locked it into her writing desk and set about her usual household chores, expecting momentarily to receive a call from Mrs. Cornfield which would enlighten her.

However, the days passed by slowly and Mrs. Cornfield did not appear. Thalia remained imprisoned in her room, refusing to speak to any of the members of the household who shouted at her through the locked door. At first Mr. Horrocks had commanded that no food should be given to her until a confession had been received, but as the days went by and Thalia remained silent, he grudgingly permitted Cook to fix her a few sandwiches which he brought up himself. Thalia wished that she had the dignity to refuse these humble offerings, but as she was feeling weak and mindless from lack of nourishment she wolfed them down before Mr. Horrocks' disapproving stare.

Mrs. Horrocks grew increasingly distressed as the days passed and there was no word from the Cornfields. Determined to discover at last the truth about the ball, she dressed herself in her finest calling costume and set out in the carriage for the Lanston townhouse, willing under the duress of these unusual circum-stances to break her vow never to cross that threshold. The Viscountess heard of her unfashionably early caller with some amazement and proceeded immediately to the drawing room, where Mrs. Horrocks was standing awkwardly before the window. Refusing the chair which was offered, she insisted that she wished some information about her daughter's conduct at the ball and would then immediately depart. The Viscountess shuddered at the word "ball" and was unable to remember much about Thalia's presence there, merely remarking that she looked quite lovely and behaved herself charmingly. She recalled an altercation in the supper room but did not know whether Thalia was involved in any way. But just as Mrs. Horrocks made her polite thank-you's and headed towards the door, the Viscountess launched into a tirade about her son's conduct, glad of this chance to complain to one who would understand her ignominy. She had been afraid to call upon her friends who had attended the ball, fearful that they were whispering behind her back about how she had been forced to allow a woman of easy virtue to become the Belle of the evening.

Mrs. Horrocks, feeling very ill at ease, murmured the appropriate condolences, marking with some inner satisfaction that her beliefs about the immorality of the upper classes were well founded. But she came to attention instantly when the Viscountess began to speak of Letitia.

"It was so dreadful," she was saying, "I am truly grateful that Letty went away immediately afterwards to stay a few days with her Aunt Catherine in Hampstead, for she did not realize at all what sort of girl Lynton had brought with him. Can you imagine, she actually walked up to her before all of the guests, and said, 'How nice to see you, Miss Stillwater.' The poor darling—she was only trying to be gracious—if she had only known—but of course no well-bred young girl could be expected to recognize that type."

Mrs. Horrocks did not wish to listen to the rest of Lady Lanston's complaints; she interrupted her quickly, saying, "What did Letty call the woman?"

The Viscountess stopped in midstream and paused to collect her thoughts. "Why, I recall plainly," she said finally. "It was 'Miss Stillwater,' though how Letty can even have known that creature's name is more than I can understand."

"But she must have met her before," Mrs. Horrocks pointed out stubbornly, "for just a little over a fortnight ago Lynton and Letitia came in your carriage to take Thalia with them to a tea party at Miss Stillwater's home. Letitia told me that Mrs. Stillwater was one of your old friends. They had just moved to London because her husband, a barrister, had found a position here."

The Viscountess stared at Mrs. Horrocks with a sort of disgusted amazement.

"Never!" she declared firmly. "I had never heard of the name until the night of the ball. I have no friend named Mrs. Stillwater, nor do I know a"—she paused and sniffed slightly—"barrister. I doubt that your information is correct. Letty has never told a lie in her life, and would certainly not accompany her brother on any such immoral expedition." She glared at Mrs. Horrocks defiantly. "Perhaps *your* daughter—"

Mrs. Horrocks, feeling the vitality of their old enmity coursing through her veins, was about to defend her daughter hotly when she remembered that Thalia had been locked into her room for crimes yet undiscovered. She swallowed her words and said stiffly, "I will be taking my leave of you now, Lady Lanston."

Once outside the door, musing over the identity of Miss Stillwater, she realized that she still had the card which had arrived with Thalia's invitation to tea. She extracted it from her silver card case and inspected it carefully. It bore only an address and Mrs. Horrocks decided to trace its owner. She directed Joseph to drive to the street in Belgravia which the card named and descended before an unimposing little residence, surely not the home of a notorious fallen woman.

The polite maid at the door informed Mrs. Horrocks that the lady of the house was out upon a shopping excursion but, if she would be pleased to accept a seat in the parlour, the master could speak with her. Mrs. Horrocks, rather proud of her detection work, was glad to take the proffered seat. Within a few moments, the man of the house entered, very much Mrs. Horrocks' image of a successful barrister with his heavy sideburns, portly demeanour, and impressive gold watch chain.

"Mr. Stillwater, I presume," she said politely.

To her surprise, the man started and became red-faced. "You must be mistaken," he said firmly. "I am Mr. Crane."

"Is this your card?" Mrs. Horrocks asked sharply, holding out the piece of white pasteboard. Mr. Crane examined it nervously.

"Yes," he said at last. "How did you come by it?"

"It was sent to my daughter with an invitation to a tea party from a Miss Stillwater," Mrs. Horrocks responded primly.

"Miss Stillwater—" the man stammered. He looked about the room nervously and cleared his throat several times.

Impatiently Mrs. Horrocks demanded, "Do you know of her?"

"Know? Miss Stillwater?" Mr. Crane sputtered, clearing his throat several times more. "Why no, I have never—that is to say, I do not...Why do you wish to know? Are you some relative, perhaps?" he ended nervously. His complexion had become so florid that Mrs. Horrocks feared he would soon go into an apoplectic fit.

"My daughter seems to be acquainted with her," she said. "I merely wondered if you knew her family."

"Family—she has no family," Mr. Crane said, hesitating and then adding, "that is, if I knew her, I am sure she would have no family."

Mrs. Horrocks was becoming increasingly irritated; it was obvious this man had information which he refused to share with her. She rose politely and was turning towards the door when the young maid poked her head in and said in a squeaky voice, "Sir, the Missus is just coming down the street."

The man thanked her with a grateful wink and, turning to Mrs. Horrocks, began to propel her bodily towards the door.

"Sir!" she cried indignantly. "I do not merit such treatment. If I could but speak to your wife for a moment—"

"Out of the question!" shouted Mr. Crane. "You must leave at once. Miss Stillwater is a—how shall I say it—personal friend of mine." His voice had sunk to a stage whisper. "I *do* know her; I know her, indeed, in the Biblical sense. Ha, ha." He poked Mrs. Horrocks in the ribs and winked wildly at this point, whereupon she drew herself up to her full height. "But you must not breathe a word of your errand to Mrs. Crane, do you understand me?"

Mrs. Horrocks merely sniffed at this and marched towards the front door, actually colliding with Mrs. Crane, who dropped her many parcels on the floor. As Mrs. Horrocks sailed on through and down the steps, she heard that lady screaming at her husband, "Who was she, Stanley? The mother of some little serving wench you have seduced? I swear to you, I would have left you years ago if it were not for the children, you and your fancy girls with their—"

Mercifully, the rest of this speech was cut off as Joseph slammed the door of the carriage and drove away. Mrs. Horrocks sank back against the seat, barely able to breathe from the horror of the moment. She fanned herself rapidly with her gloves. Mistaken for the mother of a maidservant, indeed! After a few moments of stern reflection, however, she decided that her errand was not in vain. She had confirmed the true identity and occupation of the mysterious Miss Stillwater and the thought that her daughter had visited this female brought new possibilities to her mind. Pushing them aside for the moment, she determined to call upon Mrs. Cornfield and accordingly directed Joseph to that address.

Mrs. Cornfield's butler at first insisted pompously that she was not at home, but as Mrs. Horrocks persisted, he finally muttered that there was a serious illness in the family and he would see if she could be brought down from the sickroom. Mrs. Cornfield appeared shortly, in more disorder than usual, her hair loose about her face, her large hands all aflutter.

"Florence!" she cried, descending upon Mrs. Horrocks, waving her arms wildly. "It is so good of you to call and inquire after poor dear Freddy's health. It appears as if he will be all right after all. The doctor has just left and said he can rise from his sickbed today, God be praised!"

"I did not know Master Frederic was ill," Mrs. Horrocks replied calmly.

"You did not, and yet you came," said Mrs. Cornfield musingly. "How like a good friend to know such things without words. It was that dreadful man at the Lanstons' ball, who fought with Freddy and forced him to cut his hand upon some glass. It became infected, you know, so horrible, all green and yellow. I have been a Mother for many years, as you know, and such a wound I have never seen. Why, I have gotten no sleep, these past four nights. Just tossing and turning and hearing my poor darling moaning in pain."

"I did not know that Master Frederic was injured at the ball," Mrs. Horrocks replied, hoping that her placid countenance and words would have a calming effect upon Mrs. Cornfield. "Pray, how did it come about?"

"Thalia did not tell you?" Mrs. Cornfield almost shrieked. "But of course she would not, the poor sweet girl —that odious man forcing his attentions upon her—she must have nightmares about it still."

Mrs. Horrocks merely repeated her question.

"Why, I barely recall. It was so long ago. Years ago, it seems," Mrs. Cornfield said, sighing dramatically and pressing one large hand to her forehead. "A mother ages, I warn you, when her oldest son is on his deathbed, or nearly his deathbed," she murmured. "I suppose it all began when he forced her to dance a waltz."

"A waltz?" asked Mrs. Horrocks sharply.

"Oh, you need not worry, Florence," Mrs. Cornfield protested. "I would not allow her to dance any at all, not even with Freddy, and he is almost her fiancé. But how can I have forgotten—he has not proposed yet! And you were expecting him! Of course, you understand, under the circumstances—"

Mrs. Horrocks realized that she was not learning anything. "The waltz?" she inquired politely.

"Oh yes, the waltz," Mrs. Cornfield said, startled by the abrupt change of subject. "Well, Thalia was standing with us, as sweet as could be, such a darling girl, I shall be glad to have her as my daughter-in-law. They make such a lovely pair. Ah yes, where was I? the waltz. There she was, standing right beside me (as I said before) and this horrible man came up and simply tore Thalia from my side even as I was telling him that she could not dance a waltz. And he forced her to dance with him. I could see that he was holding her so tightly the poor girl was ready to faint with the pain. And she could not break away, for it would have created such a scene. And then, before we knew what was happening, they just disappeared! He had spirited her away! Knowing how careful you are about your daughter's character, I immediately thought to myself, 'Now what would Florence do in this situation?' That is exactly what I thought. And do you know what I did?"

Mrs. Horrocks shook her head impatiently.

"Why, of course, I tried to find her!" Mrs. Cornfield announced triumphantly. "Together Freddy and I went through the entire house, from the wine cellars to the top of the attic, looking into every room. And she was nowhere to be found. And then Freddy, my clever boy, remembered the supper room and when we arrived there, what do you suppose we found?"

"Thalia dining with this man," Mrs. Horrocks suggested.

"Why, Florence! You are as clever as Freddy!" Mrs. Cornfield cried. Mrs. Horrocks winced. "That is exactly what we found. Can you imagine, the presumption of that man, thinking that because he is a Peer, he can snatch my son's escort away from him and take her to supper himself. Well, Freddy immediately informed him that he was mistaken in his choice of a partner, that Thalia was betrothed (or nearly betrothed you must admit) to him. And then do you know what that man did to my poor lamb?" She paused melodramatically and then answered her own question. "He actually attacked him, my little angel, in front of all the other guests. My brave Freddy of course defended himself, trying not to injure the man too badly, for he did not want to create a scene. But do you think the Marquis fought fairly? He did not! He pushed Freddy across the table into some broken glass, knowing that he would be injured and unable to continue. I have no doubt that he intended to kill him except that Mr. Lynton Lanston arrived fortunately at that very moment and helped to keep Freddy away from that monster's sight so that my poor darling's injury could be looked to. But that was not enough for the Marquis! Oh no! How could you expect a fiend to be satisfied with that? He actually pursued my helpless son into the drawing room and pretended to bandage his hand. Of course, that must be how it became infected, although how he managed that I do not know, but I am sure his type knows many such hellish tricks." She sank back into a chair, exhausted by this long speech.

"This man—who was he?" Mrs. Horrocks asked speculatively, hoping to get a clearer answer than the one she had received to her former question.

"I do not know precisely," Mrs. Cornfield confided. "I was told he was the Marquis of Parringdon, and I do recall, Mr.

Lanston calling him by some name—Stacey? Yes, that must be it. Oh, you could tell by his looks that he was the Devil's Own Lieutenant. Handsome, but in a depraved way. Fair-haired, bold, blue eyes—the sort of man that every loose-brained female runs after. I am sure he must have seduced a thousand women. It was fortunate that Freddy was Thalia's escort, for if he had not been there to put that man in his place, I shudder to think of what would have happened to her."

Mrs. Horrocks shuddered at the thought of what might already have happened but did not voice her suspicions to Mrs. Cornfield. She merely thanked her, asking pointedly, "And will Freddy be feeling well enough to come around to the house tomorrow morning?"

"Oh, to propose!" Mrs. Cornfield said archly. "Why, Florence, you never lose your wits, like Poor Little Me! But of course Freddy will be there—if I have to carry him myself—and I may have to, for he is still so weak. But there, I have been forgetting my duty to my poor invalid. I must rush up immediately. I fancy I can hear his pitiful cry for me now." Mrs. Horrocks could also hear this sound but privately thought it more like a bellow than a pitiful cry. "Mama!" came the shout again.

"I will show myself out," Mrs. Horrocks said firmly. "You must not trouble yourself. And we will expect you tomorrow. Mr. Horrocks will stay home deliberately to see young Frederic."

Mrs. Cornfield nodded distractedly and flew upstairs, her crumpled skirts trailing behind her while Mrs. Horrocks was ushered out into the sunshine by the formal butler. Upon the short drive home, she recalled the strange manuscript which was still locked in her desk, and after dinner shut herself into the sitting room to read it by the poor light of a candle.

Thalia's script was careless and awkward; at first Mrs. Horrocks had to pore over each page, holding the candle so close to the words that she almost scorched them. But gradually she found it easier and was deeply absorbed in the story by the time she reached the last page, which ended with Mariana's handsome young Protector asking, "Will you marry me, my darling?" Reflectively Mrs.

Horrocks arose and fed the Novel to the sitting room fire, page by page, musing upon what she had learned.

It was obvious to her that the first part of the Novel was autobiographical; she recognized her first husband, Lawrence, and his ridiculous spoiling of the child. She was quick enough to realize that the aunt in Bath and her spoilt daughter were caricatures of herself and Flora. The young Protector gave her a little more trouble but she at last thought to compare his name and appearance to that of the Marquis of Parringdon as described by Mrs. Cornfield. Thalia's hero not only bore a striking physical resemblance to the Marquis, having his curly blond hair and blue eyes, but was named (unimaginatively) the Marquis of Partington. Mrs. Horrocks knew of course that not all of the Novel could be true, but she was willing to believe the worst: that her daughter had previously associated with, and possibly been seduced by, the man at the ball.

This grim conclusion she decided must be kept secret. It was not a subject which she could discuss with Thalia and it was not a fact she would care to reveal to Mr. Horrocks, who shared her concern for maintaining a respectable front to the world but was inclined to blame her whenever one of his stepdaughters was misbehaving. If Frederic Cornfield could be brought to offer for Thalia (and this seemed very probable) then Mrs. Horrocks would see that her daughter was married as quickly as possible so that the awesome responsibility of watching over her would be at last out of her hands.

Mrs. Horrocks was not a vindictive woman but she felt a need to vent her rage and so, after watching the last page of the manuscript crumple into flame and disintegrate, she slipped quietly up to the upstairs hallway and paused outside Thalia's locked door.

"I know what you have been up to; I have read and destroyed your disgusting story and I understand All," she hissed, pausing to be sure that she had caught Thalia's attention, although there was no sound from within the room. "Frederic Cornfield will be here in the morning to ask for your hand in marriage, and you will accept him or you will be very sorry, miss." Feeling much better for having thus expressed herself, Mrs. Horrocks marched off to her bedroom.

Within the dimness of her room, Thalia was aware of her mother's words. Although she found the first part of the speech puzzling, she was encouraged by the news of Mr. Cornfield's imminent proposal, for it enabled her to set her latest plan into action. To this purpose, she was up early the next morning to watch the Cornfield family carriage pull up before the door and was already dressed in her lilac-and-cherry-striped morning dress by the time Mrs. Horrocks came to unlock the door.

They spoke little as they descended to the study, where an interesting tableau was presented. Mr. Horrocks was seated in dignity before his enormous mahogany desk, while Frederic stood before him, humble, a hat in one hand and a small wrapped package in the other. Mrs. Cornfield loomed over Freddy to the right as if she were a Guardian Angel urging him forward in the path of duty. Mrs. Horrocks, as she swept importantly into the room, positioned Thalia by Freddy's side and took her place next to her husband behind the desk. For a few moments, nothing was said. Thalia looked demurely at the carpet; Freddy squirmed under Mr. Horrocks' stem gaze.

At last Mrs. Horrocks said impatiently, "Thalia, Master Cornfield has done you the great honour of offering for your hand in marriage and your father and I have accepted his suit with pleasure. Have you anything to say?"

She glared at her daughter like an avenging eagle but Thalia knew her lines well, having rehearsed them often in the solitude of her room. She smiled up at Frederic shyly and said, "I am very happy to accept. I will be glad to be Mr. Cornfield's wife."

Freddy started visibly at this, Mrs. Horrocks peered at Thalia in some surprise, and even Mr. Horrocks had to clear his throat several times. Only Mrs. Cornfield accepted the statement matter-of-factly, beaming down upon Thalia fondly as if she had just become one of her own children.

"Then it is settled," Mr. Horrocks said uncertainly. "We need only set the wedding date."

"I think it would be wise for them to marry as soon as possible," his wife stated quickly. "Perhaps within the month?"

Again Freddy jumped a little; his mother appeared to be turning the matter over in her mind and eventually commented, "Oh, how romantic to plan a wedding so immediately. But will there be enough time for all the preparations? The gown? The invitations? The reception?"

Mrs. Horrocks soon put an end to her friend's burgeoning fantasies about the lavishness of the wedding party by saying, "It will be a small wedding. Just the two families, and we will take some refreshments here afterwards. There is no need for a gaudy display."

Mrs. Cornfield's enthusiasm was momentarily squelched, but she shortly began murmuring instead about those details which still could be extravagant. Mr. Horrocks pumped Freddy's hand vigorously and then called in Betty to bring the best brandy from the dining room. He and Master Cornfield drank a toast to the bride while the ladies sipped ratafia, also imported from the dining parlour. Even Flora was brought in to partake of the refreshments and she congratulated Thalia quite generously, thrilled by this opportunity to become more closely acquainted with the Cornfield family.

In the midst of the celebrations, Mrs. Cornfield remembered the package which Freddy had put down on the edge of the desk and began to nudge him energetically. As this had no effect, she finally leaned over and whispered loudly enough for all to hear:

"The present, the present for your bride-to-be!"

Freddy blushed and, grasping the parcel firmly, turned to Thalia for the first time, saying hoarsely,

"I wish to present you with this token of my affection." Thalia smiled faintly and accepted the sticky parcel, opening it as slowly as possible as she dreaded the sight of the contents. The gift itself exceeded her worst expectations. It was a hair brooch set in seed pearls with a design of two hearts intertwining.

"It's Freddy's own hair," Mrs. Cornfield pointed out proudly. "You see the blond strands from on top and the darker colour here underneath." She ruffled her son's hair as she spoke to illustrate the difference in colouring. "I had it done almost a fortnight before the ball. Is it not lovely? And so sentimental!"

"Very nice," Thalia murmured in a small voice. "I shall — treasure it always."

"Quite appropriate," Mrs. Horrocks said approvingly. "Put it on, Thalia. Let us see how it looks."

After a few minutes in which all three women in the room were engrossed in the process of fastening the brooch at the neck of Thalia's dress, they all stepped back to appreciate it with oohs and aahs. Thalia felt herself fortunate as she could not see it, even when she craned her neck to do so.

The little party continued for some time, until Mr. Horrocks put away his glass and remarked that it was time for him to be off to the bank. Bowing slightly to Mrs. Cornfield, he hurried out of the room, gathering up his umbrella and hat from the hall table.

It was now time for Thalia to set her latest and most daring plan into action. She did not know quite how to begin. "Ahem," she said meekly.

"The Bride, the Bride wishes to speak," Mrs. Cornfield announced, raising her glass in a salute to Thalia. She was very susceptible to the influence of spirits and was already floating in an indistinct but friendly fog.

"It—ahem—I was thinking that I will need many things for my trousseau," Thalia said hesitantly. "And there was some lovely material on sale in a shop on Regent Street." She looked about timidly. "I was hoping you would do me the favour of taking me by there on your way home. You need only drop me off; I could walk back—" she looked hesitantly at her mother who was glaring, "with Miss Mallet of course."

"There is no reason—" Mrs. Horrocks began but was interrupted by Freddy's mother.

"Why, we would only be too happy to oblige you, my dear," Mrs. Cornfield said somewhat thickly. "I must begin looking for some fabric for my dress. As the mother of the groom I am sure I am expected to be in the pink of fashion. What do you suppose would be most suitable," she asked, turning to Mrs. Horrocks. "A grenadine? A mousseline?"

"It matters little," Mrs. Horrocks said with a wave of her hand. "Thalia should not be permitted—" She paused realizing that any restriction upon her daughter's activities would sound odd without a detailed explanation. "I will take Thalia to the shop myself later in the day. There is no reason for you to trouble yourself."

"It was the grenadine which was on sale," Thalia said demurely. "Of the most lovely scarlet colour."

"Why that would be just what I would require!" Mrs. Cornfield exclaimed. "We must go at once before it is sold. Not to worry," she added to Mrs. Horrocks, squeezing her elbow fondly. "Thalia will be safe with Freddy and me."

Mrs. Horrocks smiled weakly but could not manage to prevent Thalia from sweeping out of the house under the patronage of the human whirlwind which was Mrs. Cornfield. She barely succeeded in bringing Miss Mallet down from the nursery in time to thrust the trembling and flustered governess into the carriage as it pulled away from the curb. Mrs. Horrocks could not help suffering from misgivings for some hours, but at length decided that Thalia must surely be safe from wrongdoing if guarded by the combined forces of Mrs. Cornfield, Freddy, and Miss Mallet.

Chapter Nine

*In Which Thalia Propositions the Marquis of Parringdon and
Is Conducted on a Tour of the London Demimonde*

MRS. HORROCKS' CONCLUSIONS ABOUT Thalia's safety were,
of course, proved wrong. Thalia had feared that she would not be
able to escape from the maternal solicitude of Mrs. Cornfield, but
that lady was so entranced by the fabrics she found in the mercer's
shop that when Thalia drifted away and eventually slipped out the
door, Freddy's mother did not even notice her absence, for she was
absorbed in commanding Freddy's approval of yet another bolt of
mousseline. Miss Mallet, however, was more alert. When Thalia
quickly vanished through the door, Miss Mallet, who had been
terrified by Mrs. Horrocks' vague suggestions of peril, scurried out
after her. She was unable to take the time to notify the two
Cornfields, for a quick glance confirmed that Thalia had almost
disappeared among the throngs of shoppers. Miss Mallet,
hurrying along, clutching her reticule, her pink nose twitching as if
scenting her quarry, at last caught up with Thalia farther along
Regent Street.

"Miss Thalia, Miss Thalia!" she called in her timid voice.
"What are you thinking of? Where are you going?"

Thalia, who had been surveying the traffic, turned about in
dismay.

"Oh, Mallie," she said, "I thought you hadn't seen me. You may come with me if you wish, but I warn you," and at this point her eyes danced with anticipation, "I am going to St. John's Wood."

As she had expected, Miss Mallet gasped, knowing well the implications of this suburb. Before she could recover her composure, Thalia, with a little gesture of resignation, had darted off into the crowds again.

Miss Mallet hesitated a moment, her body swaying with indecision, and when she resumed her search for her charge, Thalia could not be found. Miss Mallet did not think further than the present; she never considered returning to the Cornfields' or reporting Thalia's disappearance to Mrs. Horrocks. Instead, she spent the next several hours haunting the shops on Regent Street, heedless of the impending rain. Her frail body trembling with anxiety, she inquired repeatedly of every shopkeeper and passer-by if they had seen a young girl of Thalia's description, until they were all thoroughly disgusted with her persistence.

Thalia meanwhile continued on her journey, following Regent Street up to Oxford Street, darting through the heavy traffic oblivious of the many curious stares she received. It was beginning to drizzle as she was at last rewarded by the sight of Lady Guenevere's house, set back in its lawns and gardens, and she scampered gratefully up the walk to be ushered by the jovial butler into the warm drawing room where a large fire was blazing.

"And what can I do for you, Miss—Lawrence, I believe?" he asked, as he helped her out of her heavy, damp cloak.

"I have come to speak to Lady Guenevere on a matter of grave importance," Thalia replied earnestly.

The butler looked crestfallen. "I am sorry, miss," he said dispiritedly. "I thought you knew that Lady Guenevere is not at home. She accompanied Miss Lanston to Brighton."

Thalia was shocked by the memory of Letty's elopement, which she had entirely overlooked in her preoccupation with her own problems.

"In regards to Miss Lanston," the butler interrupted gently, seeing that she was lost in thought, "there is a letter from her for you." He walked to a side table and chose one of the letters from a pile on a silver tray.

Thalia took it in a bemused way, noting with a little smile that Letty had addressed it to Miss Thalia Lawrence. How like Letty, she thought, to remember such fine details as a friend's pseudonym in the midst of a clandestine wedding.

"I will withdraw, miss, if you wish to read it now," the butler added. "But you have only to ring for me if there is anything you require."

Thalia smiled gratefully at this and pulled open the envelope as he quitted the room. It was a long letter but an interesting one and Thalia read it over several times.

> My Dearest Thalia,
>
> We have been Married and I am so Happy! Lady Guenevere and I (for she told me she was accompanying me when she took me up at my Aunt Catherine's home) arrived here on Sunday in the Afternoon and went immediately to the Church. Lady Guenevere was our one Witness and Edward's father the Other. His Parents are so warm and loving; it makes me sad that my own are not here. They took Lady Guenevere into their house without any question, saying only that any Friend of mine was a Friend of theirs. Mrs. Crofts cried during the Ceremony and embraced me afterwards, calling me her Daughter, and telling me that she always wished for a Daughter but had only a group of fine Sons. And Edward's Brothers are very likeable, and most handsome.
>
> You should see them, Thalia, though they are all married. And their Wives are the nicest Girls imaginable. They took me aside on my Wedding Night and told me that I must not be afraid for they were sure Edward would be the Gentlest and Kindest of Husbands. But I was not frightened for Lady Guenevere had thoughtfully explained Much of What was not known to me on the Train Journey. And indeed there was nothing to fear for I am so very happy, I am sure that I am the Happiest Woman on Earth.
>
> We moved into our New Home directly and I am having such a pleasant time decorating it. We are in a great Fluster here for

127

the first Pupils are coming Next Week; Edward has been very Busy while I was yet in London and has found Five Students already. But he left the House for me as he said he did not want me to be oppressed by Servants I did not like and Decorations which did not suit I am sure I would never be able to manage but for Lady Guenevere, who has helped me find an Excellent Cook and the Sweetest little Parlourmaid. You cannot imagine what fun it is to be the Mistress of your own Establishment.

I must write to my Parents next which I sincerely dread, so adieu for now. Please write me as soon as you are able and let me know the News in London. Wasn't it Dreadful of Lynton to bring Susannah to the Ball? I know my Mother is in a Terrible Rage as a result.

With fondest wishes, I am, and will always be,

your devoted friend, Letitia Crofts.

Thalia sighed a little as she finished this missive for the third time. She envied Letty her new-found happiness but knew she could not find such benefits in marriage, particularly not if the prospective husband was Mr. Frederic Cornfield.

The memory of her own recent betrothal recalled to her the urgency with which she must carry out her plans. She determined to call upon Susannah, since Lady Guenevere was not at home, and, ringing the butler, asked him to show her out.

The summer rain was heavy now and she stood for a few moments before the gate, drawing her cloak closer about her.

At this moment, a magnificent barouche pulled to a stop before her, splattering her skirts with mud and water. From it descended the Marquis of Parringdon, who stood taking in Thalia's bedraggled appearance for a moment and then ushered her quickly inside the carriage, from which vantage she could hear him outside swearing volubly at his coachman. Thalia was not the only occupant of the barouche. Across from her sat a beautiful, young, dark-haired woman whom she immediately identified as Stacey's French mistress.

The girl was dressed in an extremely gaudy manner and was highly painted; she wore a crimson satin dress, a flimsy black cloak edged with feathers, and many costly rings upon her white hands. She was not pleased with Thalia's presence but flicked her skirts away from Thalia's muddy cloak with a disdainful air, and sniffed audibly. Her flashing dark eyes dismissed Thalia with an almost venomous glance and she turned her thin, elegant face away quite obviously, choosing to fix her attention upon the Marquis, who was stepping back into the barouche and attempting to help Thalia clean her soiled skirts.

"Stacey, *cheri*," the girl said in her high, nasal voice, "who is this creature? What is she doing in our carriage?"

"Arlette DuVannes, Thalia Lawrence," muttered the marquis, not bothering to turn about. Arlette stretched out one hand and clutched his arm possessively.

"Stacey," she said coaxingly, "it is enough that you have helped her, but she is not going to ride with us, is she?" Stacey, who appeared not to have thought of this possibility, glanced at Arlette and then back to Thalia.

"Is there someplace we can take you?" he asked in a low and comforting voice. "You looked quite lost."

Thalia, who felt like weeping, answered instead in a cool tone, "If you would be so kind as to take me to Susannah Stillwater's house, I would much appreciate it."

Stacey squeezed her hand warmly and then shouted out the directions to the coachman, who started up with a jerk, which sent them all sprawling. When they had untangled themselves, Arlette had firmly taken hold of the Marquis and had drawn him onto the seat beside her while Thalia sat gazing desperately at the floor, striving not to reveal the depths of her misery. She had not before believed in the existence of Arlette nor had she thought to find Lady Guenevere gone when she most needed her. Stacey's confident and prompt announcement of the direction to Susannah's home struck her with new questions about the degree of intimacy between him and Miss Stillwater. A glance out of the carriage window at the thickening rain only encouraged her depression.

129

The barouche jolted to a stop before Susannah's villa, and Thalia tried to slip out with a murmured thank you. But Stacey would not have this, insisting that he should usher her to the door and wait to be certain she was admitted. It was well that he did so, for Susannah's stern, sour-faced housekeeper answered their knock and would not let them past the threshold, declaring that Miss Stillwater was not at home.

Thalia's already shaky self-control crumbled. In a moment of utter despair she envisioned herself married to Frederic Cornfield and turned from the door blindly, about to run off into the rain. The Marquis, however, stopped her, taking her by the hand and informing the housekeeper that they required a few moments to dry off in the drawing room and some fresh tea. The stern woman looked down her nose at him but marched off quickly as if going to do as he had bid.

Thalia allowed Stacey to lead her into the drawing room with his arm about her waist and settle her into a comfortable chair before a large fire, while he stripped off her wet cloak, shaking it out before the flames, and chafed her cold hands with his own warm ones. She stared mutely at the fire.

"What is it, little one?" Stacey asked in a troubled voice.

"Not to trouble yourself," Thalia said quietly and meekly. Without the advice of Lady Guenevere or Susannah, she could not broach the subject of her future plans. "Arlette—" she murmured faintly, "she is outside—waiting—"

"Arlette can wait. It will be good for her." Stacey said firmly. "Tell me what worries you."

Thalia shook her head stubbornly. "I cannot," she said, in a voice perilously close to breaking.

"Miss Horrocks," the Marquis said commandingly, "the masquerade is over. I wish to be your good friend, and I demand that you trust me. Does it have to do with that young swine you are expected to marry?"

Thalia stared at him in amazement. "You know me?" she asked in astonishment. "How did you? When did you—?"

"From the first, you silly darling," Stacey said fondly. "You do not think you could deceive me with your pretty flirting airs. You were so afraid when I touched you that I could feel your body trembling."

With a gasp, Thalia remembered their conversations. "But at the ball," she interrupted, "and you called me Miss Lawrence, and you pretended that I should be your— um—" Her voice trailed off. "And you knew then?"

"Of course," Stacey responded. "But as you preferred to be Miss Lawrence, I honoured your wishes. It was an amusing game. But now that you see that I know your background, you must explain to me why a well-brought-up young miss is wandering about the London streets alone in the rain and calling on two of London's most well-known courtesans."

"A game!" Thalia cried indignantly. She felt the colour rise to her cheeks and clenched her fists. "You toyed with me as you would a child, allowing me to make a fool of myself before all of those people at the ball. Sir, you are not a gentleman! If you recognized that I was not a—um— pretty horsebreaker, it was most improper of you to treat me as one. I will not stay another moment—"

But her words were broken off by the entrance of the housekeeper carrying a silver tray with a complete tea service upon it. She slammed it down noisily upon a table and marched out again, closing the door behind her with an eloquent bang. Thalia had risen and was struggling to reach her cloak, which the Marquis held out of her grasp.

"Sit down, Miss Horrocks," he said firmly. "You are not going back into the rain and cold until you have had some tea. I can see now that I am going to have to protect you from your own worst nature."

Thalia glared at him but remained in her chair. The resentment she felt at his treatment of her had completely erased her previous depression; the promise of a verbal skirmish with the Marquis was delightful. She meekly took the cup and saucer he offered her and sipped the tea demurely, awaiting his next words.

"Allow me to tell you what I think you are scheming," the Marquis said, settling back into his chair, crossing his legs, and taking a sip of his own tea. Thalia was about to object to his presumption but was not permitted to speak as the Marquis continued. "You have been brought up in a spoilt and haphazard manner by your charming father, the late Mr. Lanston, only to find when he died that your mother would not allow you the same freedoms. She must be a cold, bitter woman, overly concerned with outward appearances, difficult for a girl of your warm and impulsive nature to understand. You determined to free yourself from what you considered a virtual prison and became acquainted with Miss Stillwater and Lady Guenevere, who seem to live happily in comfortable independence. Since at this moment something has recently occurred to upset your plans for freedom, perhaps the marriage with Mr. Cornfield, you have determined to join them in their profession." He studied her with a look of amusement, adding, "No doubt you fancy me in the role of Protector."

Thalia, who had been amazed that he knew so much of her background, blushed at this last sentence, but could not deny it. That he had bothered to inquire of her family and circumstances, that he had so well guessed at the nature of her plans, that he had so arrogantly presumed that she was interested in him (which unfortunately was true), all of these facts combined to render her speechless. She considered her various alternatives, disclaiming his words violently, or running from the room in silence, but found, to her horror, that she was beginning to giggle.

"You are an amusing little minx," the Marquis said smugly as he watched her struggle to suppress her laughter.

"Minx!" exclaimed Thalia, having found her tongue at last. "Sir, it is too much to expect that a gentleman of your type would have the grace not to accuse a lady of the improprieties which you have just named, much less speak of such matters before her. But I find that not only have you pried into my past and taken liberties with my person, but you have descended to the level of calling me by childish names. I find this conversation exceedingly distasteful. I beg leave to go."

She rose with as much hauteur as she could assume and reached again for her cloak, but Stacey artfully moved it from her, casting her off balance so that she fell against him, and he drew her down upon his knees, pressing her head against his shoulder and caressing her hair with his hand.

"I gather that I have guessed the truth," he said, in much kinder and gentler tones. "But, Thalia, it would not suit."

Disconcerted by his physical proximity, Thalia found herself fighting an urge to dissolve into tears. "Why should it not suit?" she demanded in a shaky voice. "Lady Guenevere and Susannah—"

"Are the exceptions," the marquis said bluntly. "They come from backgrounds very different from your own; they learned their trade well, with much luck and much native aptitude; they know how to manage in a world of men, how to scent danger and turn it aside, how to manipulate people to serve their own ends, how to lie, how to refuse, how to choose. In short, they are excellent business women. But even they have had to suffer from shame and cruelty and poverty. And the rest—the vast majority of the pretty horse-breakers, as you so delicately refer to them—they are miserable slaves to their need for money and alcohol, to their owners (for in many cases they are merely possessions) and to their own drives. You must never—"

At this moment his lecture was interrupted by the re-entrance of the housekeeper. "There is a young—female at the door," she said, "asking for, nay, demanding, I should say, the Marquis of Parringdon—"

"I will deal with her," Stacey said, putting Thalia gently aside and exiting quickly, ushering the housekeeper out of the room with him. Thalia heard what seemed to be an argument between the French girl and the Marquis through the closed doors, but paid little heed to it. She felt alone as she had never felt before, missing the warm enclosure of Stacey's arms, the comfort of the physical presence of the man who had called her "darling" and caressed her hair. When he re-entered the room, she saw with a fresh shock of pleasure, the warmth in his blue eyes, the elegance of his appearance.

"Arlette is leaving in a cab," he announced, resettling himself upon the sofa and drawing Thalia beside him. "And now what have you been thinking of while I was gone? Have you reconsidered your plans and recognized the truth of what I have said?"

133

Thalia blushed, remembering the direction of her thoughts, and murmured inarticulately, "I do not know. There is nothing else—I cannot go back to Russell Square."

She paused and stared into the fire, striving to collect her scattered thoughts. After Stacey's short speech the life of a pretty horsebreaker seemed more difficult than she had expected, yet it was certain that she could not write another Novel before the impending marriage with Freddy, and such a marriage still seemed a fate worse than death.

"I have no alternatives," she said finally, shrugging her shoulders a little. The marquis studied her for a few moments, then rose to his feet, lifting her also, and draped her cloak about her shoulders.

"I can see that before we decide upon your future," he said firmly, "I must discourage your romantic conceptions about the muslin company. I will conduct you on a short tour of the London demimonde, which I trust will shatter them for all time."

In another moment, he had propelled her from the room and out the front door without ever ringing for the housekeeper. And in another moment, they were seated in the barouche on the start of this strange pilgrimage.

It was a short drive to South Marylebone, an area which the Marquis claimed contained many of the higher-class brothels in the city. Thalia was fascinated with the opulence of the first house into which they entered, exclaiming involuntarily at the glittering expanses of mirrors and the crystal chandeliers, the rich brocades and the velvets and satins used for draperies and upholstery. The inhabitants were still asleep, but Stacey convinced a chambermaid, who seemed to know him well, to conduct them upstairs into some the bedrooms. The larger and more elegant rooms were deserted; maids were at work cleaning wine stains from the carpets, carrying out plates of half-eaten food which were scattered about the sofas and tables, removing the dirty bed linens and straightening the furniture. Stacey pointed out without much comment the heavy leather straps upon the posts of some of the beds. When Thalia looked at him with a question in her eyes, he muttered obliquely, "For some of the newer girls from the country who aren't willing, or for the pleasure of men who prefer young children who are bought from their parents on the streets of London." Further upstairs, under the attic, were the small, dirty bedrooms in which the girls slept. The chambermaid went along with them to open the rooms with a key. "They are locked in," Stacey whispered to Thalia, "for most of them would run away if they could. Their owner is a cruel and selfish woman; she keeps most of the profits for herself, only buying the girls their fine clothes for displaying themselves and a little gin once in a while. And yet this is one of the more exclusive brothels in London." As the doors were opened, Thalia saw young girls sprawled in thin, dirty wrappers amongst dirty sheets in airless rooms with no windows. Some of the occupants were soundly asleep, often clutching an empty bottle, and Thalia could see the dark circles under their eyes, their tangled hair, and the smudges of last night's make-up. Others awoke screaming curses, and Thalia recoiled as a string of oaths was unleashed upon her. Several recognized the Marquis and called to him, and Thalia, while struggling with the new emotions rising in her as a result of this tour, also found herself disconcerted by questions about the marquis and his obvious familiarity with the house and its inhabitants.

But she had little time to reflect upon this as Stacey swept her out of the house and into several others nearby. They seemed much the same; the deterioration from tawdry elegance to filth and poverty as one penetrated into the interior; the girls, always dishevelled, inebriated, and exhausted; the signs of bondage and servitude.

As they were leaving the third house, Thalia thought she had seen the worst of the conditions which Stacey had promised to show her, but she was not prepared for the horror which assailed her as they passed a large barren room near the back of the house and saw a group of little girls, none above the age of twelve, who were being herded like a flock of lambs along the corridor. Some of them seemed to be in a daze, stumbling as they walked, their eyes large with a look of confusion and fear.

Thalia found herself shivering uncontrollably. Stacey misunderstood this symptom and, thinking that she was cold, drew her close to his side as he guided her back into the waiting carriage. Thalia meant to question Stacey about the children, but as she turned to him, she found him staring moodily out the window at the falling rain while the carriage splashed through the streets towards a destination south of the Thames. Thalia could not command Stacey's attention until at length she withdrew a little from the shelter of his arm, which was still about her, and he turned, asking, "Are you much warmer, then?"

"Those young girls—" she stammered, "in the—last place—"

She seemed to recall him from a great distance for he hesitated a moment before answering, "Oh, yes. At Madame LaRoux's. She collects them for gentlemen who are willing to pay high prices for a girl that age. You saw but a small portion of them; there are hundreds of them that have passed through her house at one time; children that she buys from their parents or tempts away from jobs as milliner's assistants or in domestic service, promising them employment with a wealthy family. Some are kept at that house until they are no longer of use, whereupon she turns them back onto the streets; the vast majority, however, are shipped to Belgium and Germany to be kept in brothels there."

"Shipped?" Thalia asked, a tremor in her voice.

"Yes, put on ships, treated as cargo," the Marquis answered a bit impatiently. "They belong to their purchaser; they are distributed to various establishments in other countries for a handsome price, for the pleasure of foreign gentlemen who prefer English girls."

"Surely they could leave, run away—" Thalia suggested. The Marquis shrugged his shoulders, a little too callously, Thalia thought. "There are ways to keep them submissive. Many of those girls you saw were drugged. They are forced to sign contracts under duress; they are told that if they leave they will be subject to prosecution. They do not speak the language, nor do they have any money, nor suitable clothes. They have nowhere to go." He resumed his survey of the area immediately outside the carriage window. As all Thalia could perceive through the clouded pane was the continuous downpour of the rain, she was irritated by his lack of feeling.

"It is time for me to go home," she found herself saying icily. "My mother will be frantic. By now the Cornfields must have returned from the mercer's shop." Her confident, authoritative tone faltered. "I wonder," she began despondently, "what excuse I can give. I had thought never to return."

"Ridiculous!" snapped the Marquis, pausing to command the coachman to turn about. "But I have not brought you this far without showing you what I intended. Come over by the window."

Thalia obeyed gloomily. Stacey had cleared a spot on the pane through which she could dimly see that they were in a maze of dirty, narrow streets, filled with filthy, unkempt human beings who seemed to take no heed of the rain. Young girls, wearing only rags, with pitiful, pinched faces and protruding bones, were standing in doorways or running out amongst the crowds to accost the men that stalked by. They watched the barouche with greedy eyes, running up to the window, shrieking out promises and pleas in shrill, desperate voices. In the upper windows of the grubby taverns which seemed to fill the entire street, Thalia could see older women, naked to the waist, leaning out to taunt passers-by with strange oaths.

"It is difficult to fathom," Stacey said with almost a snort, "but these brothels have been here since the eleventh century at which time they were owned by the Bishop of Winchester, passing later into the hands of the Lord Mayor of London, who—"

Thalia felt his words pressing upon her like a heavy weight. She was terrified of the growing darkness, of the desperation of the women beyond the carriage door, of the violence which seemed to lurk in every dark doorway of the narrow streets, of the seeming indifference with which the Marquis spoke of these unhappy people.

"You must take me back immediately," she said in a stifled voice. She folded her hands tightly in her lap.

"We are already proceeding in the direction of Russell Square," the Marquis said, staring at her with puzzlement. "Is there something wrong? I assure you, there was no danger; of course—"

"Please do not concern yourself," Thalia said resolutely. "You were absolutely correct in showing me what you have; I shall never think of this—profession—with the same romantic notions which I must admit I had fostered. But—please," and her voice broke a little, "do not speak to me. I would rather be alone with my thoughts."

Stacey watched her with dismay as she sat so quietly and rigidly beside him, but, honouring her wishes, he turned and stared idly out the window and they completed almost the entire journey in silence.

Chapter Ten

*In Which Thalia Becomes a Journalist and Is Nearly
Imprisoned in a Brothel*

AFTER THEY HAD BEEN travelling through the growing gloom
for what seemed to Thalia an hour, Stacey suddenly commanded
the driver to halt and leaped out of the carriage without a word of
explanation.

Thalia, who had been submerged in the misery of her private
reflections to the exclusion of his presence, was abruptly brought
back to reality. She hesitantly peered around the half-open
carriage door and found to her surprise that the rain had stopped
somewhat although a heavy fog had settled with the evening upon
the city streets. So heavy was this fog that at first she did not
realize that they had stopped at the very corner of Russell Square;
it was several more minutes before she spotted Stacey, who was
ushering a tall, sticklike woman towards the waiting barouche.

"Mallie!" cried Thalia with a gratitude which surprised even
herself. She threw her arms about the bewildered governess, who
Stacey had by now forcibly conveyed into the carriage. Miss Mallet
had for several hours been roaming the area about Russell Square,
too timid to face the wrath of Mrs. Horrocks, too frightened to be
able to think of another course of action. Her joy at finding her
charge again rendered her incapable of questioning the situation in

which she now found herself; she sat quivering in a corner of the cab, emitting tiny squeaks of amazement every now and then, while Stacey and Thalia, with the relish of conspirators, planned a convincing fabrication. At length, they decided that Thalia had stopped outside the mercer's shop for a moment and fallen to the ground in a swoon. She had been carried into a nearby shop, with Miss Mallet following, and had only recently recovered from the effects of the strange malady that had overcome her. It would have seemed more appropriate if Miss Mallet had been the victim of this peculiar disease, since she still appeared to be in a sort of fit, but the confused governess made her objections to this suggestion clear by shaking her head fiercely and muttering in terror, although she was easily convinced to play her part in sustaining the alternate story. When they had rehearsed the tale several times, Thalia gratefully bid the marquis goodbye, aiding Miss Mallet from the barouche and setting off in the direction of the Horrocks home.

They entered to find a large company gathered in the parlour: Mr. and Mrs. Horrocks, Flora, Freddy, Mrs. Cornfield, and even Mr. Cornfield. When Thalia first saw the expressions of suspicion and anger upon their faces, she feared that she would not be able even to remember the deception she and Stacey had so elaborately wrought, much less impart it to those concerned. But as she spoke, assisted by Miss Mallet's total incoherence, she found with relief and a great weariness of spirit, that the dismay had turned to pity, the rage into compassion. She was hurried upstairs and immediately sent to bed with a posset of hot milk and, to her amazement, she drifted off quickly into a deep and dreamless sleep.

In the morning, Thalia found herself still treated as an invalid. She was allowed to sleep late, the apothecary was called round to inspect her (and also the inarticulate Miss Mallet) and she was brought breakfast on a silver platter. Thalia revelled in the new luxury and care although neither her mother nor stepfather deigned to enter the sickroom, sending up Betty instead to take Thalia a politely worded message that the apothecary had said she should soon be on her feet after a good bloodletting, for which purpose he would return on the morrow.

The horror of this last suggestion brought Thalia immediately out of her bed, and she presented herself dressed for supper at the family table just as dessert was being removed. She could dimly remember in her early childhood when she had been stricken with a fever, and leeches had been applied to her already suffering body until she screamed with such agony, that her father had come into the room, ordering the apothecary to take himself off and never return. Determined at all costs to prevent a reoccurrence of this nightmare, she seated herself demurely at the table, saying timidly, "I feel so much better, I thought perhaps I should join you."

So convincing was her performance that instead of being sent back upstairs, she was prevailed upon to read the selected passage from the Bible that night and then given the piece of embroidery over which she had been struggling for many nights. At first Thalia relished the domesticity of this familiar scene: her mother and sister quietly sewing by the flickering lamps, the muttering of Mr. Horrocks in the study working upon his accounts. But as she worked upon the delicate floral designs, she found the visions of the young girls in the brothel and on the streets swimming before her, and when at last she was permitted to go to bed, instead of vanishing these visions became so much stronger that she was unable to sleep, so consistently did her mind dwell upon what she had seen.

As the hours passed and she tossed and turned, trying to find some comfort in rearranging the linens or moving the pillows, a new plan of action began to take shape in her thoughts. Accustomed as she was to creating elaborate plots to enliven her tedious existence, she first viewed this new idea as a delightful yet frivolous fantasy. She saw herself upon a platform at a public hall declaiming violently the society which allowed young girls to be treated as merchandise while below her the staidly dressed matrons and gentlemen of the audience first bristled with outrage and then kindled to her pleas. Eventually this daydream was replaced by one in which an article on child prostitution by Thalia Lawrence (she once more congratulated herself upon her pseudonym) was raising a public furore, whispered over at tea parties, debated in Parliament, discussed in all the clubs. Eventually she found herself deliberating over the phrases of this essay, adapting much of her information from Stacey's words and the passion behind them from the scenes she had witnessed.

It was not until the birds began to chirp busily in the Square beyond her window and the dim early morning light began to filter through the heavy curtains that Thalia realized that this already cherished scheme could be accomplished. Since her "mysterious fit" at the mercer's shop, she had been allowed the utmost freedom of action within the house. She remembered distinctly the direction and even the exact number of the house to which Stacey had taken her. Of course it never occurred to Thalia that perhaps future research into her material need not be acquired in such a manner; in fact, it was the delicious anticipation of danger (as well as the subsequent fame) which drew her so strongly forward.

She arose dutifully, before even Mrs. Horrocks was up, behaved with unwonted decorum throughout the long, dull hours of the day, which were relieved only by the unimpressive pleasure of a morning call by her future husband and his mother. However, as soon as she had been excused from the parlour in order to retire for the night, she felt a new energy activating her tired limbs and mind. Silent as a mouse, she crept about her room, dressing herself in the most extravagant finery by the light of a candle, so that when Mr. Horrocks, the last of the household to retire, came ponderously up the stairs and closed the door of the master bedroom, Thalia was ready and slipped quietly out of the kitchen door and into the cool night.

South Marylebone was not a long distance away, and she walked quickly, glad to find that there were few people about, slipping into the shadows when a coach rolled by. As she approached the street which she and Stacey had toured, she encountered much more activity. Fortunately most of the habitués of the many establishments arrived by cab, and Thalia was able to creep up to the portal of the house during an interlude in the traffic. But once there, sheltered in the shadow of the area gate, she realized that her task was not an easy one. She witnessed several parties of men arriving; all were submitted to the most careful scrutiny by someone who seemed to be a butler before they were ushered within. Quite suddenly she was aware that two young men were approaching her, strolling down the sidewalk, although she was as yet unobserved. She was about to creep further into the shadows, when she noticed how very young and unsure of themselves they appeared to be. The older, dark-haired one was telling some anecdote about Skittles, while his companion, whose fair hair and moustache reminded her somewhat of the Marquis, attempted to laugh, but the squeak in his throat betrayed his nervousness and unease. With a flurry of skirts, Thalia abruptly stepped into their path. Still unsure of herself, she noted their reactions. The older one flinched slightly, then frowned while the fair-haired man at first started but then began to smooth down his moustache appreciatively. Boldly, Thalia took his other arm, which was tucked into his waistcoat pocket.

"Kind sir," she began, which she hoped seemed a suitable address for a woman of the streets, "would you be so thoughtful as to grant me a small favour?"

"What is it you want?" demanded his companion sharply, but the younger man continued to stare at Thalia in amazement that he had been awarded such an attractive young female.

"Certainly, my dear," he said at last, hesitantly, patting her hand as he spoke the words.

"I wish to enter this house," Thalia said rapidly, ignoring his friend and indicating the establishment of Madame LaRoux with a wave of her hand, "in your company, if you please. You see—"

"It is not usual to bring a female with you to such a place," the older man interrupted with a note of sarcasm.

"But I am sure it is sometimes done," Thalia replied promptly, knowing no such thing.

"And you told me yourself, George, you know you did," said the friend to whose arm Thalia still clung, "that Madame LaRoux is always combing London for new girls. She should be delighted to have such an attractive young woman desiring to make her acquaintance."

"You do not begin to understand the customs of London, Horace," the older man answered with a shrug of his shoulders. "But I suppose you never will. And when I said young girls, then young girls is what I meant. This one must be too old by ten years to suit Madame LaRoux. But never mind. It can be done; just be grateful that I have a special invitation, for if not, you could be sure neither you nor your fair companion would see the inside of this doorway." And so saying, he sauntered up the front steps and pulled upon the knocker.

Thalia felt a slight weakness in her knees and was glad that she was still holding firmly to her newly found prize. But within a few minutes they had passed the inspection of the pompous butler, and the cold, calculating stare of Madame LaRoux, an extremely tall and buxom middle-aged woman with an elaborate coiffure of bright red hair, and were entering a large salon full of people. At first, Thalia noticed only the men, of every age and shape, from portly business-men in striped waistcoats to languorous aristocrats in top hats and tails to several uncomfortable-looking young men who seemed to have come up from Oxford for an evening of pleasure and clung to each other desperately in one corner of the room, nervously smoking cigars. The gentlemen glanced at her in a new way, which Thalia found exciting as well as intimidating. However, once they saw that she was accompanied, they returned to their conversations with the other women, who were all, Thalia realized suddenly, subjecting her to the most painful scrutiny. They were much older than the children she had seen in the morning though not one of the group could have been much above seventeen years. The clothing they wore contrasted markedly with Thalia's costume which she had considered shocking. But these girls were bare-armed, their waists cinched in by laced belts, their breasts almost spilling over the strained material of the bodices. When they rose to move about the room or dance, their crinoline skirts darted up dangerously, with a skill born of practice, to reveal tiny laced boots and stockinged legs. They spoke in shrill, bold voices, laughed loudly, and stared at Thalia with ill-concealed hostility. Thalia clung desperately to Horace's arm and wondered about her plan; these were not the frightened innocents she had come to protect. These girls, though no doubt once tender captives of Madame LaRoux, had acquired the sophistication and cynicism of middle-aged women and clung to this air of bravado with an almost desperate pleasure.

George had seated himself next to a petulant blond beauty upon a crimson settee; Horace was being plied with drinks by a bold young maidservant. Thalia took one of these and attempted to sip it bravely though the taste made her shudder. By the time she could see the bottom of her glass, Horace had finished four and was leaning against Thalia more heavily for support. He now had his arm about her waist and was beginning to treat her with a familiarity which frightened her. She attempted to move away from him but he merely moved closer until she found herself trapped against the wall.

She wondered how long she would be able to avoid his advances, when suddenly a gong sounded and Madame LaRoux appeared before the company.

"Ladies and gentlemen," she announced, "a rare privilege is yours tonight. You are about to witness, and perhaps even participate in, an old Greek ritual, the Rape of the Wood Nymphs by the Satyrs, before the goddess Aphrodite. The young ladies who will portray the wood nymphs have already been chosen, but we are in need of several strong and—eager men to play the parts of the satyrs. Do we have volunteers?"

Thalia felt Horace stir restlessly beside her but he contented himself by bending downwards and whispering that he and she would enact the same scene alone together. Several of the men, however, came forward and followed Madame LaRoux from the room, among them, George. As the men left the room it was possible to see more of the occupants and to Thalia's horror, in the far corner of the salon, seated upon a couch with his arms about a very young, very pretty and very terrified girl, was the man Thalia had hoped never to see again: the Baron Croydon. She turned sharply to avoid his gaze, but he had already seen her and as the pageant began, she was aware that his eyes were fastened upon her. She fancied she could feel his cold stare upon the only part of her body which could be visible, her profile and her neck where the dark curls parted.

She was barely able to concentrate upon the spectacle before her. The curtains dividing the drawing room were opened to reveal Madame LaRoux, in the role of Aphrodite, reclining upon a couch with only the flimsiest of veils about her. Encircling her were a group of the little girls Thalia had seen in the morning. All appeared dazed by their surroundings, all were dressed in transparent gowns in the Grecian mode. Madame LaRoux delivered some sort of speech, filled with apostrophes to the Muse and Jove. Thalia could not concentrate upon her words, torn as she was by both her fear of the Baron and by her pity for the children. The closest little girl she could see was trembling, her large, baby-like eyes dark with incomprehension. Upon the striking of a large gong by Aphrodite, the gentlemen entered the room clad only in breeches, with leering satyr-masks over their faces. With much enthusiasm, they began to clutch at the young girls who broke from their poses and ran in genuine terror. The assembled spectators began to laugh at some of the ludicrous occurrences: a fat satyr becoming stuck as he tried to pursue one of the unwilling nymphs behind a couch, another man trying to kiss his struggling prize without removing his mask. However as the proceedings became more wild and abandoned, dresses were torn away and masks and breeches discarded, Thalia found herself running out of the room in sickened revulsion.

Fortunately, the entire company, including the servants, were watching the scene in total absorption and not even Horace noticed that she had slipped from his side. The cool darkness of the passageway was a relief after the bright lights and obscene noises coming from the drawing room. Thalia paused a moment to collect her wits, and then finding a back stairway, followed it up past the bedroom floors to the very top of the house which she knew must be near the attics. Tiptoeing down the unlighted hallway, Thalia could not say what had drawn her to this part of the house, but she soon realized that she had come to the correct place. Behind the closed doors, she could sometimes hear the chatter of young girls and, once or twice, a broken sob. She pressed herself against one door, rattling the knob, but it was firmly locked. The conversation from within ceased immediately.

"Who are you? Are you in there? Do you want to come out?" Thalia whispered desperately. There was a moment's silence.

"Who are you?" came a timid little voice from behind the door.

"I am a friend. I want to free you," Thalia answered with conviction. She tried to project her sympathy and concern into her voice. "If you want to be free, I can help. But you must tell me how."

There was another long silence, then a whispered consultation within. At last the same voice responded, "We are locked in. Only the scullery maid has the key. Do you know why we are here? Do you know what She plans to do with us?"

Thalia ignored the questions. She had very little time. "I will be back," she whispered quickly, and, turning about, sped down the stairway. Once on the ground floor she ferreted out the kitchen. To her relief, all of the servants seemed to be off, undoubtedly watching the scene in the drawing room. After a short search, during which she paused frequently to listen for footsteps, she found a ring of keys hung upon a nail near the stairs. Again she made the ascent, again she wandered down the narrow corridor, trying to recall which door she had stopped beside. She was strongly aware of the alcohol she had consumed; she had seemed to glide down the stairs and along the hallways, but now her fingers fumbled as she tried key after key into the lock.

Just as she thought she had the correct key at last, she heard loud voices from another part of the same floor.

"I cannot imagine what she would be doing here," declared a shrill female voice.

"Nor can I," answered a seemingly familiar male voice, with a trace of coldness and cynicism in the intonation of the words. "But I swear I will pay you a large fortune if you find that girl for me. I have been searching for her throughout all of London's nighthouses. To think she was here, and with that besotted young fool, only to slip away."

Their voices were rapidly approaching the hall in which Thalia stood. Almost without thought, she found the key turning beneath her slippery fingers. Desperately she pushed the heavy door open and sliding through it, let it shut behind her, sinking to the floor with relief.

Looking up she saw four little girls standing before her, their eyes wide with amazement. They were barefoot, dressed in cotton nightgowns. The one who seemed to be the oldest, being about eleven or twelve, stepped forward and said bravely, "Who are you? What do you want?"

"Hush!" whispered Thalia violently. "Do you hear the voices? They are looking for me. Be silent."

The voices were indeed very near, in fact they seemed to be just outside the door. Thalia could no longer distinguish their words, but she could picture with absolute terror Madame LaRoux and the Baron Croydon discussing her in the hallway, for she knew by this time who the speakers were.

Suddenly there was a grating at the door behind her back and, like a rabbit running for cover, Thalia dashed beneath one of the iron cots, lying huddled in the dust, painfully aware of every sound. She could hear the door being thrown open, the little girls pattering towards one bed on quiet feet, Madame LaRoux saying in an overly loud voice, "Have you heard anything? Has there been someone in this hallway who should not have been there?"

There was no sound from the children. Thalia hoped they were shaking their heads. She heard the baron's heavy tread moving towards the other side of the room, then his voice saying, "This one is charming, is she not? I should like to make her acquaintance. How soon can it be arranged?"

"You fool," Madame LaRoux responded with a trace of annoyance. "We are here chasing another girl for you. Shall we discontinue our search? I have a thousand such girls like the one you have your hands on. If you wanted one, you had only to say so. Dragging me up all of these stairways, disrupting the play—"

"You know that the play is still going on without you," the baron interrupted with condescension. "No, you are right. I have no taste for these trembling little beauties tonight. It's that other girl I want, the wild one. She bit me the first time we met, at Cremorne, when she was with Susannah Stillwater. And then later I saw her at Lady Guenevere's gathering. She must be a common drab, but I have not been able to find her since."

"Go ask Susannah, or your precious Lady Guenevere," Madame LaRoux retorted. She began to move from the room.

Thalia felt, rather than saw, the baron hesitate. Then he also left, saying, "You know that Susannah has not admitted me to her house for nearly a year, and Lady Guenevere was pretending to be the girl's mother. Having given up her own, I suppose she feels the lack. She would not be likely to—"

The door shut behind them.

Thalia lay in the silence for a moment, breathing deeply, suddenly aware that the keys which she still clutched in her hand were cutting her fingers. Finally she noticed that the little girls were crouched beside the bed, peering in at her.

"I'm coming out," she said briskly, and wriggled forward and into the centre of the room, where she leaned against the bed, listening to the sound of other doorways being opened and shut, until the noises and the voices finally died away. She relaxed suddenly, her shoulders sagging, and when she reopened her eyes, she found the children watching her as if she were a fairy godmother materialized from a fairy tale.

"Can you take us away from here? Who was that mean woman with no clothes on? Do you know why we are kept locked up?" the eldest girl said, all in a jumble.

Thalia responded by asking another question, "How did you come to be here, and why do you think you are here?"

"I am here," the outspoken girl said, "because this was the address of a house which advertised for an under-parlour maid. I came to apply and talked to the lady with the red hair in a grand drawing room, and she said I would suit and brought me up to this room. She gave me something to drink—we still have it sometimes in our night-time milk— that made me fall asleep. And when I awoke, the door was locked. Since then, we see only the maid who dresses us and takes us down for breakfast, and then another maid who brings our supper. None of us know exactly why we are here, but some think we will be sold to men for their pleasure. Is that true?"

Thalia paused a minute before responding. "Yes, it is," she said slowly, "though most of you, I have been told, will be sent to the Continent to be put in brothels there."

The girls looked at each other with a mixture of incredulity, interest, and fear.

"Does she have any right to keep you?" Thalia asked.

The same child spoke again. "Not I, for I was tricked into remaining here, but many, like Susan," she pointed out a very frail, painfully thin girl, "were bought. Susan is from a big family of twelve children, and her mother couldn't care for them properly, so when Madame LaRoux offered her ten pounds for Susan, why, her mother could not refuse it."

Thalia started slightly, and Susan spoke up. "I know she loves me, miss, but we were desperate. I'm sure I could not have better food or pretty clothes as I have here, and I have not been poorly treated."

"And how many others are there?" Thalia asked solemnly.

"In all, at least forty, I guess," the outspoken girl replied. "What will you do?"

"I intend to leave," Thalia said. "I still have the keys. And if any of you wish to come with me, I will bring you to a safe place where you may stay for a while and then decide what it is you wish to do." She wondered for a moment what she would do with them, but went on with conviction, "After the house is quiet, we will release the others and ask them if they wish to come."

"It will not be till dawn," one child said. "We often hear loud noises all through the night, although no one comes with our breakfast until nearly noon."

Throughout the night, Thalia and the four occupants of the room traded information about the practical workings of the household, particularly the floor plan, and by the time the sun had risen, Thalia, along with the boldest of the little girls made a rapid tour of the hall, explaining the true nature of Madame LaRoux's establishment and her plans for them and offering a promise of escape and a haven. Nearly half of the children, in all about twenty-five, were eager to leave; the rest either declared, like

Susan, that they had never lived in such luxury, or were as suspicious of Thalia as they were of Madame LaRoux.

This entire process consumed over an hour of that precious commodity, Time, and Thalia was faced with the further problem of how to conceal twenty-five little girls dressed only in cotton nightgowns, for they were given no other garments. Leaving the chosen group sitting in a huddle at the top of the stairs, she went below to reconnoitre. There was no one stirring about the house, and she made her way quite easily out through the kitchen entrance to discover an alley behind the house which would serve her purpose well. Going out onto the main thoroughfare, she managed to flag down two cabs and directed them to the back. Then she flew up the stairs and shepherded the little girls down through the house and out through the stable yard into the alley where the carriages were drawn up, both drivers having a cigar and speculating upon the mysterious purpose of the young female who had requested their services. They were further mystified by the sight of the children being stuffed into the two coaches by Thalia. She was, at this point, quite a sight, with her hair loose about her shoulders, her flimsy dress covered with dust, barking out orders sharply and gesturing wildly.

Once the last of the little girls was safely hidden in the interior of the cab, Thalia turned to the two open-mouthed men, curtseyed quite respectably, and said sweetly, "If you gentlemen would be so kind as to start up immediately. My cousins are very anxious to be back home."

One of the drivers shrugged and took up his seat at the reins; the other paused for a moment and then followed suit. Thalia's story was patently absurd, but another did not readily present itself to mind.

"Where to, miss?" shouted the first driver, and Thalia, who was taking a seat on the box beside the other cabbie, gave him the direction of Lady Guenevere's house.

Thalia felt very smug and self-satisfied, driving along in the early morning air, her hair flying about her face, her skirts flapping in the wind. She still could not believe that her plans had gone so smoothly, but she saw the cab ahead of her carefully threading through the back streets towards Saint John's Wood, and she heard the giggles and chatter from within her cab. It was time for self-congratulation, she decided.

As they rounded the last corner before Lady Guenevere's house appeared upon their right, she realized that she was still clutching the ring of keys, and threw them away from her onto a nearby lawn, delighting in the sparkle of the metal as it arched through the air.

Chapter Eleven

*In Which Miss Stillwater and Mr. Lanston Become Betrothed,
It Is Revealed That Mrs. Horrocks Is Not Thalia's Mother,
and the Marquis Frees a Bear*

THE LETTER FROM LETTY, informing her parents of her elopement, had gone unopened for many days. Lord Lanston had set it aside when he saw that it came from a Mrs. Crofts, for he assumed that the mother of his recently dismissed tutor was writing to upbraid him. He wished to put the whole unpleasant episode out of mind as soon as possible; unfortunately, when he at last opened the envelope and read the contents, it was brought most forcibly to his attention.

Shouting for his wife, he left the study and took her from her guests in the drawing room. Lady Lanston dissolved into tears at the first few lines, and read the remainder of the missive with trembling hands and tear-dimmed eyes. The guests were ushered out by the butler, and a passionate discussion took place in the study. Lady Lanston insisted that Letty be forgiven and received back into the bosom of the family; her husband just as firmly declared that no daughter of his would behave in such an outrageous manner and that she was to be cut off from all communication with her relations.

At this unpropitious moment, Lynton strolled in to announce offhandedly his engagement to Miss Susannah Stillwater. The ensuing battle lasted many hours and ended without any satisfactory conclusion. Lynton, feeling the force of Love was on his side, argued that Letty should be permitted to marry anyone she chose, as he intended to do. The Viscountess asserted that the family reputation would be destroyed, that Lynton could not possibly understand what ridicule he would bring upon his innocent siblings. The Viscount felt that Lynton's liaison with Miss Stillwater had been a good joke at the ball, but was no longer in good taste. He warned his son that Susannah would mistreat him, take his money, and then leave, witness the case of Mad Wyndham and Mrs. Willoughby, which had been in all the papers a few months before. It seemed that Mad Wyndham, so named for his exploits at Oxford, had married Agnes Willoughby, one of London's most highly paid courtesans, as soon as he came of age and then settled on her a perpetual income of fifteen hundred pounds a year. Horrified, his uncles had called for a Commission of Lunacy to determine that he was not of sound mind and therefore not able to squander his fortune upon such a woman. Young Wyndham eventually won his case, but Mrs. Willoughby left him two months after the marriage.

Lynton was incensed at the suggestion that Susannah was equally mercenary, but much of his rage stemmed from the unpleasant truth that he himself doubted her. He, in fact, had not yet proposed to her, and stormed out of the Lanston mansion, determined to confront her with his plans.

She received him in the dining room, dressed only in a silk wrapper, where she was finishing a lazy breakfast, surrounded by a flock of cats to whom she threw occasional scraps.

"Susannah," announced Lynton, settling down heavily upon one of the delicate chairs and trying to ignore her attire and the lateness of the breakfast, which reminded him of other unpleasant facts, "I want you to marry me."

Susannah paused in the process of putting a piece of buttered toast into her mouth.

"But, Lynton, whatever for?" she asked.

"Because I love you, and I cannot live without you. I want a house with you in it, and children perhaps. You can even bring all of the damned cats. I want you to be my wife," he said earnestly.

"But, Lynton," Susannah answered, realizing at last the seriousness of the topic and putting down the toast. "I enjoy my present life. Well, if I do not precisely enjoy it, at least I am comfortable. I do what I please, when I please. I have a lovely home, I—" her voice faltered, and she looked upon him sadly.

Lynton looked dismayed. "You know how I feel about you; I thought perhaps you also—"

"Yes," Susannah answered quietly. "I feel very differently about you than any other man I have known. I would like to live with you. I would like to have your children. I am sure we could be very happy. But marriage— marriage is out of the question. Whatever would your parents say?"

"They have already said it," Lynton confessed, revealing the discussion of the morning. Susannah laughed and chided him for telling his parents of his intentions before informing her, but inwardly she felt distress and panic. She had decided against marriage many years before, knowing that most of her patrons were married men, learning from their conversations that most marriages simply deteriorated with the passing of time. Yet for many weeks, she had been unable to prevent herself from daydreaming about becoming Lynton's wife. She thought of waking with him in the morning, of eating breakfast together, attending parties together, paying bills, discussing acquaintances, etc. She tried her new name, Mrs. Susannah Lanston, caught herself gazing fondly at small children, and found that she was watching with new interest every married person who came into her life. During their conversations and time spent together, she had learned to care for Lynton more deeply than she had believed possible. He seemed to encourage her and praise her for all of the qualities which others had ignored, while she had seen him grow from an immature and spoiled boy into a serious, thoughtful, and tender man who derived more enjoyment from people and life.

Her reflections were halted by the awareness that there was an increasingly awkward silence. Lynton was gazing at her with puzzlement, as if awaiting an important answer. Susannah strove valiantly to recall his last words but could not

"Lynton, darling," she said, putting out her hand and covering his own. "You have cast me into a state of great confusion. Allow me a day to think over this question, and I will give you your answer tomorrow."

Lynton sighed, shrugging his shoulders like one who has lost an important battle. Leaning over to kiss her lips, he murmured, "I will be here early in the morning," and then, hat in hand, took himself sorrowfully away.

Susannah found that she could not finish her breakfast, and while dressing for the day, pondered what she should do. In the case of such an important decision, she realized she could not rely upon herself alone, for her own thoughts and desires were in too great a conflict. She at last determined to seek the advice of Lady Guenevere and set off immediately.

The lady had just returned from Brighton and was engaged in supervising the unpacking of her belongings when Susannah was announced, but she quickly came down to the drawing room to entertain her guest, directing the maid to bring coffee and some cakes to the front room.

Susannah and Lady Guenevere discussed for some little time the details of Letty's elopement, for Susannah had learned of it from Lynton, and Lady Guenevere was happy to explain her own part in it and the pleasures of staying as a guest with the Crofts. But she soon realized Susannah had not come on a purely social call, and, putting down her coffee cup with a gracefully resigned manner, she asked if there was something troubling Susannah.

Immediately Susannah poured out the story of her love for Lynton and begged advice about marriage.

Lady Guenevere listened quietly and, when Susannah's tumbled explanations had ended, said softly, "I cannot speak for any other but myself. However I was once in a similar position, and if you would be interested to hear my story, perhaps it can shed some light on your own."

Susannah nodded her assent and Lady Guenevere began. "Many years ago, when I was four or five years older than yourself, and was living under the protection of the Duke of Rollinleigh, I met a young man at a party who affected me in much the same way your young man seems to affect you. For a time we had a quiet affair, then we both realized the pain we were causing to ourselves and others, and I left the duke's patronage, and my lover found me a little house on the outskirts of town. He was the second son of a prominent family and did not have much money, as his father kept him under close watch, although he was also known about the city for his carefree life. However, that was before we met. For almost two years we lived a life of domestic bliss. I own that phrase seemed odd to me at the time, and still does, but it is true, even though it does not acknowledge the terrible battles which occur when one lives day and night with another. Yet during that time, we learned to love each other more. He did not visit any other woman; I had left behind entirely my previous way of life, for this man alone satisfied both my mind and my body as no man has done since. This idyll, as I have come to look at it, came to an end when I discovered that I was with child. He was delighted, but I had never desired children, I suppose because I still feared that someday I would have to return to my former occupation and a child would be a burden to me then. We had terrible battles. I insisted that I would give the child up when it was born. He stormed out of the house. Two weeks later, I learned that he had abruptly married a rich man's daughter with whom his parents had been trying to match him. He took up his wild life again, although I remained in semi-retirement and avoided the places I knew I would meet him. Just a week after my baby was born, he reappeared, demanding the child. He had convinced his wife to raise it as her own, and I gave up my baby willingly, for I knew she would be well treated. He said little of his wife, but I knew throughout their marriage that he was miserable. He was involved in several famous scandals and drunken brawls, frequented the lowest night-houses and gambling hells, although it was said he adored his little daughter and kept her by him constantly. Many years ago, he died; his wife disappeared and, along with her, our daughter. Sometimes I long for that child, but I know it was my own foolishness that ruined my happiness. We are led to believe that happiness cannot last, that all joys are transitory, but that does not give us the right to pass up the joy we find, as I did. Perhaps we would have ended by hating each other, but now all I know is that I ruined both his chances for happiness and mine."

At the end of this speech, her voice had broken, but her dark eyes remained clear, though fixed tragically upon Susannah as she recounted her story. Susannah was deeply moved and found it difficult to speak. At length she said, "You have helped me more than I could have imagined. You are right, it is only cowardice that is holding me back. I truly wish to marry Lynton, and there is only one manner in which I can discover whether such a marriage will work. But there are so many practical problems. What of his parents and how they will treat me?"

Lady Guenevere smiled and began to recount several anecdotes about women she had known who were in Susannah's position. They were totally absorbed discussing these details and planning the wedding, when the maid rushed into the room without knocking, a look of terror on her face.

"'Scuse me, mum," she said abruptly, "but there's a man with a bear on the front step, demanding that I let him in."

"A what?" questioned Lady Guenevere.

"A bear," came a cheerful voice from the hallway, and the Marquis entered the room jauntily, holding a chain which was attached on the other end to a large, battered-looking bear. The animal's claws clattered on the stone of the passageway.

"Take that beast outside immediately," Lady Guenevere directed, rising and pointing in a dramatic gesture towards the back of the house. "You may leave it in the garden for the moment, for the fences are secure, but mind you return to us with some magnificent explanation for its presence when you return."

Stacey bowed obligingly and departed. They could hear the bear's claws scuttling down the passage. Within a few moments the Marquis was back, striding confidently into the room and pouring himself a glass of sherry from the tantalus on the sideboard.

Lady Guenevere spoke not a word, but merely fixed him with her large, dark eyes.

"I suppose you are wondering about the bear," Stacey said agreeably, settling himself on the sofa beside Susannah. Neither woman made any reply.

"Why, it's quite simple," he informed them, pausing to sip from his drink. "A young lady of my acquaintance, who, in fact I had the pleasure to meet in your gracious company," he bowed slightly to Lady Guenevere, "by the name of Thalia Lawrence, informed me that she wished to have that bear. It has taken me almost a fortnight, but I have at last convinced his owner to part with him, for an outrageous sum, I might add, and I thought that I would keep the bear here until I can present it to the young lady, not having room in my townhouse, you know." He smiled innocently and took another sip of his sherry.

Lady Guenevere was about to deliver a scathing speech upon his arrogance and lack of breeding, but was interrupted by Susannah, who said excitedly, "Oh, Stacey! The most exciting news! I am to marry Lynton Lanston, Thalia's cousin, you know."

Stacey lifted his eyebrows, smiled broadly, and patted her knee fondly, saying, "Congratulations. I know Lynton only slightly, but I am certain that you two will—"

His felicitations were halted by Lady Guenevere's uncharacteristically harsh outcry. "What did you say? Thalia is Lynton's cousin? Thalia Lawrence, the girl who was here?"

"Oh, I've given away her pseudonym," Susannah said ruefully. "She is the child of Lynton's Uncle Lawrence, the one who was the rogue of the Lanston family. Her mother, from what I hear, is a dreadfully vulgar little woman, who—"

But this last sentence went unheard, for Lady Guenevere had slipped gracefully to the floor in a faint. Instantly the guests were galvanized into action. Stacey dashed out the door, calling for the maid. Susannah searched desperately for a vinaigrette of smelling salts, but could not find such a condescension to frailty anywhere in the room. At last she also ventured out into the hallway and, taking up a peacock feather from a vase, held it in the flames of the fire and began waving it back and forth under Lady Guenevere's nose. Stacey, re-entering with the cook and the maid, wrinkled his nose in distaste at the smell, tossed the charred feather aside and poured instead a small glass of brandy which he forced between Lady Guenevere's lips.

At last the lady's eyelashes fluttered and she drew herself up, refusing support, as if ashamed of her weakness.

"You cannot imagine," she said brokenly. "I have never done such a thing before—but my daughter—my own lost, lovely daughter—Lawrence's child—under my very eyes— here in my own home—the wonder of it!"

Susannah and the marquis stared at each other. "Thalia?" Susannah inquired at last.

"Yes," Lady Guenevere sighed, falling back on the sofa in a languid pose and clasping her hands before her. "Susannah, surely you have not forgotten the story I just told you. That man, the one I truly loved, was Lynton's uncle, Lawrence. He married a dreadful Cit's daughter, a fat, unhappy woman—"

"Mrs. Horrocks," the Marquis said in amazement. "But she remarried, a banker, by the name of Horrocks. Then Thalia is not her child. It is no wonder—" His words trailed off.

"No wonder what?" Lady Guenevere demanded. "Is she happy? Is she treated well? What was she doing here, posing as Thalia Lawrence?"

"She leads a very unhappy life," the Marquis informed her seriously, though Susannah was making little gestures at him, knowing full well the depth of Lady Guenevere's compassion and devotion. "Her mother—or rather, her stepmother, is quite cruel to her, does not seem to understand her nature, keeps her shut in the house. In fact, she was so miserable that she was thinking of embarking upon a career as a pretty horsebreaker. Luckily I met her accidentally and put an end to all such foolish notions."

"And how did you accomplish this?" Susannah said quite coldly. Her hands were on her hips; she faced the Marquis, who was still standing, as if they were combatants.

"Why, I took her on a little tour of the demimonde," Stacey replied in a perplexed way. "It was all quite simple. Just showed her some brothels, for instance, Madame LaRoux's, and a few streets in Southwark, told her a little about their lives."

160

"Simple!" shouted Susannah, her creamy complexion flushed with pink. "You are simple. She's a sweet, sensitive, very delicate girl. She should never have been exposed to such things. Surely a few words, a gentle warning would have sufficed."

"But she was quite convinced about her desires," the Marquis said in some confusion. "Neither you nor Lady Guenevere were about. She came to enlist your aid. And I was unable to persuade her with words. I assure you, I would not have taken her on such a tour if it were not a desperate case. But to see a refreshing and brave girl like Thalia, the sort of girl I have been searching for all of my life, insist that she wants—"

"And why have you been searching for this sort of girl?" Susannah inquired provocatively.

"Why, I'd like such a woman for my wife," Stacey said. "It is so rare that one finds that charm, that vitality, so often missing in the simpering Society misses."

"If you wished to marry her," Susannah said despairingly, shaking her head at the folly of men, "then what prevented you from asking her?"

The Marquis paused for a moment. "Why, the thought never occurred to me," he said at last. "You see she had thought of me as one of her patrons, once she was set up in business. And that would have hardly been the right time to propose marriage. And then again, her parents. I knew she was already betrothed to someone of their choosing, and it's doubtful they would approve a match with me under any circumstance. Of course, now," he nodded at Lady Guenevere, then tried to resume his explanation. "The bear, also. You see, I knew she wanted the bear, and I thought perhaps after I gave it to her, there would be a time when we could—"

His words were cut short by a knock at the drawing room door, and the maid entered to announce, "Mr. Lynton Lanston." No sooner had the words left her lips than Lynton burst into the room, his coat askew, his hair rumpled.

"Susannah," he called, proceeding directly towards her, with barely a nod to Lady Guenevere and the marquis. "I know that I promised I would not speak to you again before tomorrow, but the most dreadful thing has happened. And so shortly after Letty's elopement. My cousin Thalia has disappeared. I thought perhaps she might have come to you."

For a few minutes there was total pandemonium. Once it was explained that Lady Guenevere was Thalia's true mother, and Susannah gave Lynton the answer to his proposal, which occasioned several kisses, the Marquis demanded to know the story of Thalia's disappearance.

"Mrs. Horrocks sent a note round to our house, which arrived just after I left this morning," said Lynton, "for your house," here bestowing several kisses upon his betrothed. "It seems that Mr. Horrocks arose in the middle of the night, having heard the noise of a door closing below stairs. He investigated and discovered that the kitchen door was ajar. A further search revealed that Thalia's room was empty. They looked about the neighbourhood for her as much as they could at that late hour, but there was not a trace. She had left no message; only one dress and her cloak were missing. It appeared as if she intended to be gone for only a short time. And yet she has not returned. I thought perhaps I might find her here. Where else could she be?"

"With Letty?" Susannah suggested. "But surely she would have taken a valise, and not set off in the dead of night."

"Has she any other friends?" Lady Guenevere inquired.

"None but my sister, as far as I know," Lynton replied.

"I'll wager it has something to do with that tour you took her on," Susannah said, turning on the Marquis. "If she is in any sort of trouble because of your foolish, unthinking, fatuous—"

There was again a knock at the drawing-room door.

Chapter Twelve

*In Which Thalia Is Disowned, Adopted, and
Betrothed All in One Day*

"LADY GUENEVERE," THE MAID said hesitatingly, stepping shyly just inside the door, "there is a young lady and about twenty-five little girls—dressed only in nightgowns—outside. The young lady wishes me to pay for two cabs, and the drivers are being very nasty. They say it is a havey-cavey business, and they will not let her come in. And, ma'am, I have never seen any of them before in my life!"

"Thalia! It must be Thalia!" shouted the Marquis, pushing the maid aside and running out of the room. Before the others could arise, he was back, his arm about Thalia's waist, and followed by the children, who grouped silently about Thalia as if they were ducklings and she their mother.

"Where have you been? What has happened? Where did you find these—" Lynton asked, waving his hand at the little girls. "Your parents have been frantic."

"It is quite a long story," Thalia said with a new-found composure. She looked about at her flock with maternal solicitude. "The girls are very hungry. Do you suppose," she looked sweetly at Lady Guenevere, "that your staff would be able to find them some sort of breakfast?"

163

"Certainly," Lady Guenevere answered in a subdued voice, trying not to gaze too hungrily upon the countenance of her long-lost daughter. She directed the maid to take the children into the dining room, which she referred to as the "refectory." Thalia whispered a few words to them and patted them affectionately as they left in a troop. Their excited young voices could be heard as they pattered down the hall behind the maid.

"Who are they? Where did you find them?" asked Susannah impatiently. "Where have you been all night, Thalia?"

Thalia settled herself in a chair. "At Madame LaRoux's," she said demurely, with a sideways glance at the Marquis, who was standing beside her.

"I warned you, Stacey!" Susannah declared passionately.

"But she is safe, is she not?" the Marquis demanded, with a fond look for her. "My brave, foolish girl, why did you go there?"

Thalia looked meek, but a gleam of amusement danced in her dark eyes. "After that tour on which you led me," she said to Stacey, then turned to the others.

"We know of it. Go on," Susannah said curtly.

"I began thinking about what you said," Thalia continued, again addressing the Marquis, "and I decided that someone must make all of the facts about such places known to the World. Of course—"she looked appealingly at the others "—it is known to many, but I mean the General Public. I thought perhaps if I could write an article exposing many of the evils which Stacey—er—Lord Parringdon—pointed out to me, and if the article was accepted by a magazine, that perhaps something could be done about— well, for instance, about those children you saw with me. They were locked up and drugged, but I am getting ahead of myself. I determined to go to Madame LaRoux's and try to speak to some of the children and learn about how they were treated. So I slipped out of the house at night and walked there, gaining admittance with two young men who were going in. There was a play, or a spectacle—at any rate it was a diversion—and I found my way up to the attics where the children were kept. I talked to some of them, and together we formed a plan to escape, so I brought as many with me as I could, and came here."

She finished her story with a little helpless gesture of her hands, as if she realized there were many omissions but did not know quite how to explain them.

"Thank God, you are safe!" Susannah said, shaking her head in amazement and glaring angrily at Stacey. "Madame LaRoux is a very unscrupulous woman. If she had found you there, if she knew now—"

"I was almost caught," Thalia explained sheepishly. "It seems a man there—you know him, Susannah, the Baron Croydon—was interested in me, and persuaded Madame LaRoux to search for me. But they have no idea who I really am. He thinks I am a common..."

"Pretty horsebreaker?" suggested Stacey helpfully.

"A drab," Thalia responded with a smile. The entire company laughed for a moment at the disjunction between Thalia's previous innocence and her new worldliness. Then the Marquis said quietly, "I think perhaps you also do not know truly who you are. Lady Guenevere has an important matter to discuss with you, and I think we should leave you alone together for a time."

"We will go to the library, Thalia," Lady Guenevere said, rising gracefully and holding out one slender white hand.

Thalia rose to join her with almost equal grace, and as they left the room Susannah noted with amazement how closely the two resembled each other. She and Lynton and the Marquis discussed the remainder of the day, creating and discarding various plans until it was decided that Lynton and Susannah would go together to the Lanston mansion to announce their betrothal, while Stacey would be entrusted with the task of delivering Thalia back to the Horrockses.

Some twenty minutes later, Thalia and Lady Guenevere returned, arm in arm, both plainly delighted with each other. Thalia seemed transformed. The new confidence she had shown upon entering the house had blossomed forth even more strongly. Her eyes shone, her lips curved upwards, almost irresistibly, an inner source of light seemed to glow through her skin. In demeanour, she no longer carried herself as a child, timid, meek, apologetic, but she stood upright, facing Lady Guenevere with the friendship of an equal, coming forward graciously to greet Stacey who was alone in the drawing room, Lynton and Susannah having departed for the Lanston home.

As she held out her hands in welcome to him, the Marquis noted that she had already adopted Lady Guenevere's special elegance, as if she had at last stepped into a role which suited her perfectly.

"Stacey," she said warmly, "I do not wish to do so, but Lady Guenevere—"she blushed "—that is, my mother, thinks it wise that I return immediately to my family and explain my absence. Would you be so kind as to take me there?"

Stacey nodded wordlessly, amazed by her new womanly poise.

"I am faced with the joyful but terrifying prospect of entertaining those little girls," Lady Guenevere said affectionately, gesturing in mock helplessness. "For so long I have wanted children. Now in one day I have my own daughter back, and with her she brings twenty-five little homeless girls. Thalia, my dear, what shall I do with them? Do you suppose they would be interested in the music room? I have a harpsichord, and a harp, and—"

"I am certain they would be delighted," Thalia said, giving her mother a light kiss upon the cheek. "I would be. But I shall help you with them as soon as I return. Should we go now, Stacey? I fear this will be exceedingly unpleasant."

"I would like to be with you," Lady Guenevere said with a worried frown, "but I am sure that my presence would be a debit and not an asset."

"I shall manage," Thalia said buoyantly. "I do not believe anything could dishearten me now." And she swept out of the room almost floating, the Marquis scurrying behind.

During their drive to Russell Square, Thalia chattered away without pause, recounting in detail her adventures of the night before and the topics she and Lady Guenevere had discussed, so that the Marquis found it impossible to interject more than an occasional "Hum" or "How odd." He strove to remain alert to Thalia's conversation while at the same time pondering how to approach the Horrockses with their missing daughter. It would not be an easy task, he feared, to inform a mother that her daughter had spent the night in one of London's most infamous brothels, nor that the girl had just discovered that her true mother was one of London's most well-known courtesans. But all of his fears were small in comparison to the torrent of abuse and outrage which fell upon the pair as they entered the Horrocks household.

The entire family was gathered in the drawing room, where Mr. Horrocks was engaged in describing his missing stepdaughter to the local constable. As Thalia came into the room upon the arm of the Marquis of Parringdon, Mrs. Horrocks rose, clutching the arm of her chair, her face florid, and shrieked, "Arrest that man! He has Seduced my Daughter!"

"Why, no," said Thalia innocently, stepping confidently forward. "He has only brought me home. He—" but her words were drowned in the general uproar.

Mrs. Cornfield arose from a seat behind Mrs. Horrocks and screamed dramatically, "It is Him! The Devil Himself! The man at the ball who kidnapped Thalia and tried to murder my poor Freddy!"

Not to be outdone, Freddy, who had been sitting beside his mother, stepped forward and announced boldly, "Sir, I challenge you. A duel for the lady's honour!"

The marquis looked down at Freddy with ill-concealed disgust. "Duelling has been outlawed for many years," he said quietly, with a significant glance at the constable. "I suggest you withdraw your comments."

Freddy coloured and slunk away, taking up a seat on the couch beside Flora, who gazed at him with adoration.

The constable, a broad-shouldered, mild-tempered man, seemed puzzled. But as both Mrs. Horrocks and Mrs. Cornfield were pointing at the Marquis and shrieking hysterically, he felt something must be done.

"Sir," he said politely, coming to stand before Stacey, "do you have any answer to these charges?"

"Certainly," Stacey replied coldly. "The young lady has been in my company only for the last hour. There are witnesses who will vouch to that fact."

"And last night?" screamed Mrs. Cornfield, who was enjoying her melodramatic performance.

"Last night," the marquis began slowly. He looked at Thalia, who gave him an amused grin. "Last night, the lady spent at Madame LaRoux's, and there are other witnesses who can attest to that."

"A brothel! Oh, the Shame! The Disgrace!" cried Mrs. Cornfield, collapsing in a heap upon the floor. As all present ignored her swoon, she soon raised herself enough to watch the rest of the proceedings.

"Is this true, Thalia?" Mr. Horrocks said, speaking to his stepdaughter at last. His voice seemed calm, but Thalia was acutely aware of the intense rage and hatred beneath the coldness.

"Yes, Mr. Horrocks," she said tentatively. "But there is an explanation."

"No explanation will suffice," he said icily, his anger showing a little in the trembling of his voice. "You have been gone all night, we are told you were at a brothel, you are brought home by a dissolute man of scandalous reputation, who claims he did not find you there—"

"He found me at my mother's home," Thalia interrupted, speaking quite as coldly as Mr. Horrocks.

"Your mother's home?" Mrs. Horrocks asked at last. Her hands were clenched into fists, though she was unaware of this fact.

"I was at the home of Lady Guenevere," Thalia stated simply, turning to Stacey a little, as if for support. "Lady Guenevere, who was the mistress of my father, Lawrence Lanston; Lady Guenevere, whose child I am."

Flora's eyes were round as saucers. Mrs. Cornfield forgot that she had swooned and said sharply, addressing Mrs. Horrocks, "Florence, it cannot be. Lady Guenevere is a harlot, a kept woman. Thalia cannot be her child. Why if so, then she is not legitimate. And Freddy—my Freddy— was going to marry her—" She swooned again. This time it appeared to be genuine, and Freddy got up to minister to her.

"Mama!" shrieked Flora. "It is not true?"

"Hush, Flora," her mother said impatiently with a distracted look. "You are truly my daughter. But—"

"But I am not," Thalia finished calmly. "It is so plain to me now. Why didn't I see it before? No wonder you treated me so harshly, watching at every minute to be sure—"

"You come from tainted blood," Mr. Horrocks interrupted fiercely. "The child of a rogue and a harlot. Who knows what evil you could be plotting? How much sorrow and anxiety you have caused Mrs. Horrocks? How you could have poisoned my innocent children with your deceitful ways? But it shall not happen. I shall not permit it to happen, for, I promise you, you shall never cross my threshold again. You are not a child of mine. You are not a child of this house. Go with your fancy man, back to the painted woman who is your mother. I am certain she will find you useful in her home. Be gone from here at once!"

Thalia blanched but stood painfully still.

"Harold," pleaded Mrs. Horrocks, "I promised Lawrence. I promised him that I would look after her as if she were my own child."

"She has another mother now," Mr. Horrocks announced coldly, folding his arms, "and a young fool to pay her way too, by the looks of it. Your obligation is finished, should have been finished long ago, if you had taken my advice. She could have been sent away to a convent school where they would have disciplined her properly, if you had heeded my counsel. What did your first husband ever give to you that you should feel a duty to him now? He stole your money. He brought scandal to your name. He was flagrantly unfaithful throughout your marriage. And his daughter is just like him. We are better rid of her."

"Thalia, we should leave," the Marquis said quietly, stepping forward and taking her arm. But Thalia remained rigid, staring at Mrs. Horrocks, who had covered her face with her hands.

"Harold, I cannot. I promised," she murmured brokenly.

"Florence," her husband said sternly. "Your promise is through. If that—that—brazen creature comes crawling back into this household, pretending to be a dutiful daughter, I shall take my children and leave. Think of Flora! Think of our children! How can they raise their heads when such a scandal is revealed?"

Mrs. Horrocks rose stiffly, as if she were an automaton, and, coming over to Thalia, kissed her stiffly on the cheek, murmuring, "I have tried so hard, but I could never love you as I should." So saying, without turning to face the company, she walked slowly from the room, only adding in a low voice as she neared the door, "Harold, I will abide by your opinion."

As her figure retreated from view, all eyes were fixed upon Mr. Horrocks. He shifted uncomfortably but said stoutly, "I have said all that I am going to say on the matter. If you wish to take some of your clothes and other belongings with you, fetch them now."

Thalia looked at him in amazement for a moment, then turned abruptly to go. She was halted by an outcry from another part of the room. Turning, she saw that Miss Mallet had been seated in the shadows by the front windows.

"Sir," spluttered the indignant governess, stalking up to Mr. Horrocks with her awkward gait. "You are a Monster! I have witnessed many horrible parents during my years as a governess, many incidents of cruelty and contempt to children, but never, I repeat, never, have I been confronted with such a cold, such a callous, such a pompous, such a monstrous tyrant! There is no need for you to ask me to leave. I tender my resignation on the spot." Miss Mallet marched over to Flora, who along with Freddy and Mrs. Cornfield was watching this scene as a fascinated audience, and kissed her fondly. "Goodbye, Flora dear," she said, "I shall miss you. You have always been a sweet, obedient girl and I am sure you will make someone a fine wife very soon."

Freddy blushed at this, for he found he was clutching Flora's hand.

"Thalia," Miss Mallet said, turning her back on the company imperiously, "will you be so kind as to wait for me in the coach? I have a few things I should like to bring with me, and then I will leave with you." She strode defiantly from the room. Her steps on the stairs were firm and loud, unlike her usual timid patter.

Without further conversation, Thalia and the Marquis left the house. From the carriage, they saw the constable leave a few minutes thereafter, doffing his hat in some embarrassment to Mr. Horrocks and then scurrying away as fast as his feet could take him. This sight at last liberated Thalia from her stony silence, and she burst into tears. Stacey tried to comfort her, but it was Miss Mallet, when she appeared a few minutes later with her bulging portmanteau, who had better success. She gathered the weeping girl into her arms, rocking her back and forth, and calling her by her pet childhood names. The journey back to St. John's Wood was completed in this manner.

Once they were admitted to the house, the Marquis and Miss Mallet, who was surprisingly unintimidated, explained the events of the afternoon to Lady Guenevere while Thalia was taken upstairs and put to bed. Despite her grief, she fell at once into a deep slumber that lasted far into the morning. The Marquis took his leave, promising to call on the morrow to inquire after Thalia's health. And Miss Mallet and Lady Guenevere had a tête-à-tête about Thalia's upbringing and the care and feeding of the twenty-five little girls, who were asleep, two and three to a bed, in all of the guest chambers of the house.

The Marquis, as soon as he drove off, remembered that he had not taken the opportunity to present Thalia with his unusual present, and wondered if perhaps the bear would help to rouse her from her grief-stricken state.

To his amazement when he returned the next morning, he found Thalia at the head of a game of leapfrog which was being carried on in the drawing room. She leaped up, curls flying, eyes shining, when he entered, and taking him by the hand, led him to the back parlour where Lady Guenevere, whom she shyly called "Mama," was instructing several of the little girls in the art of needlework, from whence they proceeded to the music room where Miss Mallet was rapidly inculcating a dislike for the pianoforte to a small group of pupils by banging vigorously upon the keys.

"We do not know what to do with all of them yet," Thalia confessed, bringing the Marquis back out into the hallway, where he playfully covered his ears and grimaced at the sounds issuing from the music room. "We hope to find positions for most of them in domestic service, or restore them to their parents. Most probably Letty would be grateful for help with the school. But you told me you had a present for me. Where is it?"

"In the garden," the Marquis said, with a broad grin.

"The garden?" questioned Thalia, giving him a provocative side glance. "What can it be that is in the garden?"

"If it has not escaped," the Marquis said nonchalantly, drawing her close to his side and leading her out through the conservatory down a slate path. The sun was out, although the grass was still wet from a night rain. The light glittered upon the raindrops left on trees and bushes.

"Are you feeling much better then, darling?" the marquis inquired with concern, holding her close to him for a moment and studying her face.

Thalia withdrew her eyes from his glance and looked down at the ground, moving a little out of his grasp. "Yes, thank you," she said quietly. "It was very painful yesterday to learn that I was not loved, but it also released me in some way from my unhappiness; I think I shall learn to understand—Mr. and Mrs. Horrocks—and how very hard they tried to do what they thought was best for me. And at the moment, I have everything I have ever desired, a beautiful home, the love of my mother, the freedom I have always craved... Actually, I can think of nothing more I require."

"Nothing?" asked Stacey, with a strange note in his voice, but at that moment Thalia shrieked and ran from his embrace.

"The Bear! The poor, darling Bear!" she shouted, racing across the lawn towards the mangy animal, which was lumbering about at the end of a chain attached to the stables. She swooped upon it as if it were a little child, but the bear seemed not to mind. It ignored her for the most part, after snuffling about her hands to discover if she had brought any food.

Stacey followed more slowly, and when he reached her, Thalia was petting the bear ecstatically. She turned to him, her eyes glowing, then blushed as she remembered the previous circumstances under which they had discussed the bear.

"How can I ever thank you?" she asked, with a knowing smile.

The Marquis looked at her quite seriously, taking her hands in his own, and Thalia felt suddenly ill at ease. Had she said something wrong?

"By saying that you will marry me," Stacey answered solemnly, gazing down at her with devotion.

Thalia felt a tremor of shock and pleasure shoot through her body. "You are joking of course," she said, trying to be flippant and avert her face from his serious gaze.

"Never more sincere in my life," the Marquis responded evenly. "I know I've said this badly, too suddenly, and all that. But surely you must know that I am attracted to you, have been ever since the night I saw you posing as a medieval princess with your hair loose down your back."

Thalia trembled a little and would not look up as she said, "But surely there are many other women—Why would you choose me?"

Stacey shook his head a little in amazement. "You do not realize do you, little goose, what a rare treasure you are? After years of having simpering Society misses paraded in front of me, timid, stupid, plain, and listening to them chatter away about refreshments and the difficulty of finding good servants, I meet a woman with courage and charm and wit and intelligence and beauty and eagerness to taste all there is in life, and you wonder why I would want to marry her."

Thalia met his eyes at last, but her own were troubled. "And then," Stacey added, trying to interject a light note into the conversation, "you certainly need someone to watch over you."

Thalia rallied and responded, "I freed myself quite competently from Madame LaRoux."

"True enough," the Marquis admitted amiably. "But that leads to another matter—I need your assistance."

Thalia looked at him with a question in her eyes.

"I have been searching for a writer," Stacey continued, "to help me in a campaign I have been waging in Parliament for some time now. This past year two bills were presented which would have helped prevent the sort of abuses to children which you witnessed at Madame LaRoux's. Both lost, but I am certain it was because the public was not aware of the true facts. If together we could use the research I have done and present a series of such articles, I am sure there would be a change."

173

Thalia seemed not to have heard the major part of this very unromantic speech. "Then you were not familiar with those places, because—" she hesitated.

"My darling!" cried the Marquis, clutching her more firmly. "You feared that I frequented every brothel in London nightly! And you were jealous! Oh, it is too good to be true! No, I went there simply to watch for violations of the law, although my pose was that of a patron—"

"And Arlette?" Thalia interrupted.

The Marquis shrugged his shoulders. "Arlette left me after that day we kept her waiting in the rain. I found her wandering about Portland Square, hungry, diseased, completely penniless. I brought her home with me, fed her, took her to a surgeon. She amused me for a while, and she knew much about the white slave trade, which she was willing to tell me in return for my friendship. But she has gone back to France, no doubt to marry her childhood sweetheart there. She was part of an exchange shipment of girls from abroad who were lured to England with promises of employment and then sold to brothel keepers here."

Thalia seemed mollified, but still considered him hesitantly.

"Will you marry me then?" the Marquis asked.

"To help you write your articles?" Thalia countered, her eyes dancing.

"I am certain," the Marquis responded, pausing for a long kiss, "that we will find other things to amuse us besides that."

"It might be an excellent solution to several problems," Thalia said at length, the thoughtful mood of her face contradicted by a wicked gleam in her eyes. "It would mean that we could employ several of the little girls."

The Marquis kissed her again.

"And we would have a house with a garden for my Bear," Thalia added a few minutes later.

"Certainly," Stacey murmured, gathering her to him for another kiss.

"I suppose you have as pleasant a house as Lady Guenevere," Thalia said when he freed her again.

"If you do not like it," the marquis responded, "I suppose I shall have to find you another. But of course, we could always live in sin. It seems the idea of marriage disturbs you."

"Oh, no," said Thalia, laughing, her arms reaching out for him. "I love you, Stacey, and I will marry you." She placed her arms about his neck, and standing up on tiptoe, drew him to her for another kiss.

About the Author

Waverly Fitzgerald first wrote *St. John's Wood* back in 1976 when her name was Nancy Fitzgerald and she was living in LA and working for the Los Angeles County Museum of Art. In 1981 she moved to Seattle, changed her name, and worked as an administrative assistant and finance manager for many non-profit arts organizations, including the Seattle Art Museum and the literary arts center, Hugo House. With her friend Curt Colbert, she has written five humorous mysteries featuring a talking Chihuahua under the name Waverly Curtis. *Dial C for Chihuahua* is the first in the series published by Kensington. She is also the author of the nonfiction book, *Slow Time*. She currently teaches writing classes for Hugo House and online for Creative Nonfiction and has returned to her first love: historical fiction. To learn about her current projects, go to her website at www.waverlyfitzgerald.com

An excerpt from Mayfair

To read the first chapter of Waverly's second historical romance published by Doubleday in 1978, turn the page.

Chapter One

The Initial Skirmish

TWILIGHT. The end of a dreary, grey day in late February. The rain had been falling since early morning on the great city of London.

A brownish mist, composed of the ever-present smoke which hung over the city and the moisture of the clouds, shrouded the streets. Dimly through this fog, one could make out the figure of a lamplighter going about his rounds, muffled in a greatcoat. The wheels of the carriages squelched as they rolled along the muddy avenues, bearing great ladies returning home from afternoon calls to prepare for an evening at the theatre or conveying portly businessmen to their residences after an arduous day in their East End offices. The lights in shop windows were extinguished and the shades drawn, while fires blazed in kitchens and were kindled in drawing rooms in preparation for the entertainment of dinner guests. Within the Houses of Parliament, another long-winded Lord delivered a speech in favour of the troublesome Ecclesiastical Titles Bill while his fellow peers groaned and settled down a bit more comfortably into their seats. In Berkeley Square, the viva-cious and quick-tempered lady of the house cursed at the dress-maker delivering a gown which had been ordered the day before for tonight's special reception, because though the seamstresses had worked round the clock without rest they had not had time to apply the gilt tasselling that had been requested. Several young swells peered out of the windows of Carltons laying bets on the frequency with which passers-by would slip and fall on the pavement; the tallest, youngest, and handsomest of the group consistently won, but spent his earnings on another round of brandy for his friends. In a dainty house in Mayfair, a beautiful, young woman laughingly dismissed the crowd of admirers who had spent the afternoon lounging in her drawing room, heedless of their protests about her cruelty in sending them out into the inclement weather. Throughout the city, the populace scurried, hurried, dashed towards shelter or scrambled into a waiting carriage as if terrified of contact with moisture, except in the crooked lanes and narrow courts of the rookeries, where the ragged urchins continued to run through the puddles barefoot for want of any other place to be.

And the great drops of rain continued to fall—on the lone pedestrian attempting to circumvent the worst of the puddles as on the shiny barouches of the leaders of fashion, on the great West End mansions as on the leaking roofs of the hovels in St. Giles and Seven Dials, on the flock of frightened sheep being driven down Park Lane on their way to market as on the steaming, exhausted pair of chestnuts drawing a ponderous and mud-spattered coach down Upper Grosvenor Street.

The coachman of this particular equipage peered out from the box and muttered to himself.

"One, two; three," he mumbled. "Aye, they said it 'ud be the third house on the left, but why be there so few lights? 'Twould be a pity if nought was ready, the young ladies havin' travelled so far an' all today."

He shook his head, commanded the horses to stop, and slowly descended from his perch on the box. The rain streamed off his greatcoat in rivers as he limped stiffly towards the strangely deserted-looking mansion and pulled at the knocker on the front door with all of his might. He repeated this last action twice before the door swung back to reveal a very small, very timid, and very grimy maidservant clutching a candle.

The coachman harrumphed and said, "It be the Misses Merrell, come up from Sussex they have today, and sore in need of a warm welcome." Clouds of steam issued from his mouth along with these words.

"Oi'll get the missus," squeaked the little maid and scuttled off down the corridor, a corridor that presented a bleak vista to the coachman who feared for the comfort of his employer's daughters, for there was not a stick of furniture or a lamp burning in its dank, dark recesses

Yet, he reflected, the young ladies would doubtless be eager to leave the cramped confines of the carriage, and accordingly, he retraced his steps and threw open the door of the coach. Lady Sibilla was the first to exit, leaping down gracefully and racing towards the open door of the house, followed immediately by her three pet dogs. The coachman shook his head at the sight of these beasts. Nothing but a bloody nuisance, he considered them, what with having to stop every few hours to give the dogs a chance to exercise, but then Lady Sibilla had refused to leave Partridge Park without her pets. Her stubborn insistence had encouraged Lady Sophia, who was not so scatterbrained as her older sister, and she had brought along her large, striped tabby, Marmalade. The coachman had predicted dire consequences for this melange, but Marmalade, now cuddled in his mistress' arms as she slowly descended the carriage steps, was too old and too lazy to be perturbed by the presence of any number of his arch enemies. He merely blinked his bright, yellow eyes once as Sophy paraded sedately up the walk and into the house.

The coachman feared for the safety of the last occupant of the carriage who had been locked up with this menagerie for the past day, but she scrambled to the door and sprang to the ground in a flurry of petticoats, as irrepressible as an India-rubber ball.

"Thankee, Jem," she said, kissing him lightly on the tip of his nearly frozen nose, and danced away to join the young ladies. Aye, they would miss her sorely in the servants' hall, he thought sadly, for Peggy was the darling of the Partridge Park staff with her high spirits, sparkling Irish wit, and cheerful good will. He didn't doubt that the young farmer with whom she had been walking out would miss her also, but then a maidservant with Peggy's beauty and charm should certainly find a better catch in London, perhaps even a shopkeeper.

He expected that there would be some sort of reception provided for the three visitors by the time he had unloaded the many trunks and portmanteaus and deposited them in the hallway, but even the little maid with her one pitiful candle had not returned. The three dogs were not displaying their usual curiosity but were pressed in a sorry huddle on the cold marble floor, and Marmalade, still cradled by Lady Sophia, was crying, a thin, plaintive cry that echoed eerily in the barren hallway.

"Can it be that we've come to the wrong house?" asked Peggy, bending down to comfort the dogs.

"They said it 'ud be the third house from the left, and this be it," the coachman answered in a rumble, taking off his rain-soaked cap and scratching his head.

"Oh no," said Lady Sibilla, who was lost in the shadows at the end of the corridor, although her light confident step could be heard. "I remember the house from Nell's wedding. But what have they done with all the lovely furniture? You remember, Sophy, the grandfather clock, and the oak cabinet with the fancy carvings?"

"Of course," replied Lady Sophia, in her frail, baby-soft voice. "You hid there when we played hide and seek, and we could not find you, Sibil. But where is our aunt? Do you suppose she has not yet arrived?" Her uncertain words trailed away.

Sibilla returned from her exploration, her slender form emerging gradually out of the gloom.

"Why, there's a light in this room," she said, throwing open a door that was midway down the abandoned corridor, and thus she was the first to see Aunt Lucy.

It was a bizarre scene that presented itself to her eyes, and even the courageous Lady Sibilla was thrown aback. She had discovered the dining room, but it was a room as inhospitable as the entry hall. No paintings or sconces relieved the sombre oak panelling of the walls. The chandelier was muffled in swathes of holland, looking like a giant cocoon attached to the ceiling. And the long oak table and its companion chairs were also shrouded in sheets. Only at the far end had a small space been cleared away, and there, with the light of the single lamp falling upon her forbidding countenance, sat Aunt Lucy, obviously interrupted in the task of consuming her solitary supper.

The flickering light distorted that lonely figure, so that Sibilla could gather only a fleeting impression of a massive black bulk, like the body of a monstrous spider, attached somehow to two short and ponderous arms that clutched a knife and fork, and the whole surmounted by a disproportionately tiny head which seemed to contain only a pair of very dark and heavy eyebrows, two hooded eyelids, and an enormous hooked nose. The small, pursed mouth was barely apparent, except when it opened, as it did now, to reveal a cavernous black hole, surrounded by long, horselike teeth.

"One of my nieces, I assume," said this mouth, as Sibilla watched aghast. "I thought I told you to wait in the drawing room." It was an ominous, booming voice, that filled the empty room like a death knell.

"I'm afraid you've made a mistake," said Sibilla, stepping forward boldly, though all of her instincts told her to retreat.

Mistake was a word that Aunt Lucy had never heard applied to her own formidable personage. She frowned.

The back door which led to the kitchen flew open with a bang and the untidy little maid came pattering into the room.

"Oh missus," she said in her squeaky voice. "Cook 'as pas't out on the floor, an' oi cain't rouse her, no matter what oi do, and the young ladies 'as arrived. Oh!" she concluded as she saw the dim figure of Sibilla at the far end of the room.

"So they have," returned her mistress, removing her gaze from Sibilla and fastening it upon her plate once more. "Show them to the drawing room!"

The maid came scuttling down the length of the table and whisked past Sibilla like a small, brown mouse. With one last amazed glance at her aunt, Sibilla turned and left the room.

Frantically, the servant girl had flown across the hall and was scrambling about the opposite chamber, lighting a few oil lamps and throwing dusty holland covers from the settees and chairs they concealed. This room seemed to be the depository for all of the treasures the house had formerly contained; clumps of furniture smothered in sheets stood scattered about. Pictures and mirrors, masked by wrappings of newspaper, were stacked against the walls. From the shadows of a distant corner, Sibilla could hear the hollow tocking of the grandfather clock. Sophia and Peggy and the coachman had followed her to the door and stood on the threshold looking about in wonder.

"So gloomy," murmured Sophy.

The dogs snuffled up to Sibilla, who patted them on their respective heads with an air of abstraction.

"Sure, and it could be a mausoleum," Peggy added, springing forward to help the maid in her task, but jumping back in mock terror as she uncovered a life-sized statue of a stern Athene brandishing a sword..

"We would like a fire, please," said Miss Sibilla in a grim voice, addressing the maid, who bobbed a hasty curtsey and pattered out of the room.

"Are ye sure ye'll be all right?" asked the coachman, lurking still at the entrance, torn between his loyalty to the ladies and his fear that the owner of the house would discover him in the heart of the mansion, an unpardonable sin for a mere coachman.

"Oh, Jem!" cried Peggy, flying down upon him with a comfortable hug. "I'll care for Miss Sibil and Miss Sophy. Never you mind about us. We'll manage somehow, I expect."

The coachman shook his head again, donned his still-dripping hat, and backed out of the room. The snap of the door closing behind him sounded like the bang of a coffin lid.

"Oh Sibil!" Sophy sighed. "I feel faint." She loosed her grip upon Marmalade, and fell down upon a dusty couch, pressing one plump, white hand against her forehead.

"Don't be ridiculous, Sophy!" her sister retorted unsympathetically. "You've always been perfectly healthy, and this is not an appropriate time to indulge in hysterics!"

"As appropriate as ever will be," commented Peggy gloomily, surveying the shambles before her. "Whatever is going on here, Miss Sibil?"

"Confound it if I know," Sibilla replied. "I daresay we'll find out shortly, but let's make ourselves comfortable until then."

And so it was that when Mrs. Lucy Pleet, after devouring the last crumbs of her dinner and savouring the last drops of the port wine, condescended to cross the hall to welcome her nieces, she found a very domestic scene.

A blazing fire had been started on the hearth. Huddled about the cheerful flames, an oasis of warmth and brightness in the dreary room, were the following:

One large Irish wolfhound, Oscar, who was quite the size of a small lion, and who lifted his head and snarled as Aunt Lucy paused on the threshold.

One reddish-brown fox terrier, known as Muffin, who jumped up and quivered, all of his fur standing out on end.

A spotted retriever, called Slow, who continued to sleep with his head in the lap of a young lady, dressed unobtrusively in grey merino with a white linen collar and cuffs, but whose thick mane of curly dark hair and startling grey eyes, fringed with dark lashes, did not seem those of a servant.

There was a large, hostile cat with orange eyes, who was sheltered in the arms of another young lady, clearly a gentlewoman, who was curled up before the fire, in a delicate dress of white tulle, her blond ringlets shining like gold. She seemed much younger than her eighteen years as she lay there asleep, her rosy cheeks cushioned by her hands, her pale, pink lips parted to reveal pearl-like teeth.

And finally, there was Sibilla, whom Aunt Lucy had already seen, but not quite like this. She was watching the fire from the depths of a winged armchair, and the soft glow made her ivory skin seem translucent and illuminated her large dark eyes. Her fragile colouring and oval face were set off by the thick halo of smooth, dark tresses wound about her head, and further enhanced by the delicate lilac shade of her silk gown. In short, she was a beauty, and this was a possibility that Aunt Lucy had not anticipated.

"Come, Muffin!" Sibilla called in her low rich voice, and the high-strung little dog bounded towards her outstretched hand, inadvertently stepping upon the cat in his haste. Marmalade was aroused in a trice, which awakened Sophy, who clutched at him just as the large striped creature charged Muffin. The sight of the enraged cat struggling to reach her, terrified Muffin, who made an abrupt about-face and jumped into Peggy's lap, where Slow was sleeping. The usually placid retriever, who had been peacefully dreaming of green fields and rabbits, awoke with a shock and bit down hard on Oscar's tail which happened to be directly in front of him. Yet Oscar bade no heed to this affront to his dignity, as he continued to snarl at the intruder.

In a few moments, the commotion had subsided, and Sibilla, glancing at her aunt, found her not quite so intimidating as before. In truth, she felt a twinge of pity. Mrs. Pleet was dressed in the severest mourning, from her jet earrings to the black crape ruching which finished her black wool gown, yet Sibilla knew that Mr. Pleet, whose dour face looked out at her from a brooch pinned over his widow's heart, had been dead for more than eight years. His relict, it seemed, had assuaged her grief with food and drink, for she was a massive woman with upper arms as large as hams, and a bosom that swelled forward like the prow of a battleship. As Sibilla had noticed earlier, Mrs. Pleet's head was small in comparison to this ocean of flesh, although it betrayed evidence of the same appetites; her small black eyes were almost buried in the plump dough-like expanse of her face, but the two fierce black eyebrows above them seemed to have taken upon themselves the function of expressiveness.

At the moment they were low on her forehead, and almost met at the top of the massive nose. Sibilla guessed that this grimace connoted displeasure, which suspicion was corroborated when that booming voice fell upon all of them, quelling even the dogs with its cold tones of domination.

"These creatures!" said Aunt Lucy. "Where did these creatures come from?"

For a startled moment, Sibilla thought perhaps her aunt was referring to herself and her sister, then realized she meant the pets. The wolfhound continued to snarl, adding a tone of persistent menace to the scene.

"Quiet, Oscar!" Sibilla called to him softly, whereupon he settled back down upon the hearth, continuing to eye Aunt Lucy warily.

"Stand when in the presence of your elders!" snapped Aunt Lucy. "I see that my sister has failed, as expected, to instill any sense of good manners into her daughters!" It still rankled Mrs. Pleet that her younger sister had married some seven years before she had finally caught the eye of Mr. Samuel Pleet, a wealthy Yorkshire mill owner. This was a marriage of desperation for the twenty-nine-year-old spinster, and she was bitterly aware that she had married beneath her class, just as she was bitterly aware that her younger sister's marriage to the present Earl of Corrough had been a love match. It was a source of immense satisfaction to her that the Earl and his Countess remained on their Sussex estate, unable to garner enough rents from their properties in England and Ireland to bear the enormous expense of a London Season for their youngest daughters, while she controlled the late Mr. Pleet's immense fortune and had condescended to invite her two nieces to stay with her in London. She preferred to forget that the house in which they were gathered was Corrough House, which the Earl had been forced to let for ten years, but which he had graciously loaned to his sister-in-law for her daughter, Lucinda's presentation to Society. Lady Sibilla and Lady Sophia were merely ornaments which Mrs. Pleet hoped would aid Lucinda in her conquests by providing her with invitations to gatherings where plain Miss Pleet would not have been welcome on her own.

With this thought in mind, Aunt Lucy reviewed her nieces, as a captain reviews his troops. Both girls had risen awkwardly at her command and stood—or, as Aunt Lucy thought, lounged—before the fire.

Lady Sibilla was the taller of the two, with a slender, graceful figure, long white hands, on which a tiny amethyst ring glinted, and a classically beautiful face framed by her luxurious dark brown hair. Aunt Lucy noted every detail as she paced back and forth—the fiery, one might say, defiant, look in Sibilla's dark eyes, the elegant curve of the neck, the subtle colouring and flattering cut of the lilac-striped gown which gave Sibilla an air of composure and worldliness beyond her nineteen years of age.

This one would definitely be trouble, Aunt Lucy thought. "Stand up straight, miss!" was all she said, as she passed on to study Sophy, who was flushed with embarrassment at her aunt's harsh corrections. Sophy hated disapproval of any kind, and she trembled a bit under Aunt Lucy's fierce scrutiny. Much more easily managed, Aunt Lucy said to herself, noting that Sophy would not meet her gaze and that her demeanour was shrinking. And yet despite Sophy's timid posture, it was evident that this girl had the sort of beauty so in vogue in fashionable drawing rooms; her complexion was as white as Parian with a wild-rose colour in her cheeks, her eyes were large and blue, and her blond hair fell in soft ringlets about her face. Slighter than her sister, and with a pleasing roundness of form, she had a babylike quality which Aunt Lucy hoped extended to her disposition. If so, she could be easily quelled by a word or glance of authority, whereas Sibilla would require entirely different tactics. Mrs. Pleet could not yet determine what those should be, but she had never surrendered or retreated thus far in the battle for her daughter's future happiness, and she knew she would not fail now. It enraged her that her two nieces were so lovely, but although initially this seemed a problem, her calculating mind was already seeking a way to turn this to her advantage.

Having finished with the two sisters for the moment, she faced in another direction.

"What is this?" she asked in tones of distaste, glowering at Peggy who stood in the background patiently, contemplating the fire.

"Peggy Banks, ma'am," the girl replied cheerfully in her clear, rich voice.

"Curtsey when you address your superiors," Aunt Lucy said abruptly, "and always call me Mrs. Pleet."

"Yes, ma'am, Mrs. Pleet," and Peggy bobbed quickly, continuing to look directly at the older woman with her large, grey eyes and never losing her serene smile.

"Can she be"—Aunt Lucy hesitated and almost spat out the last word—"Irish?" She could not entirely be blamed for her disgust; the Irish were the lowest race in England at the time, and advertisements for servants usually finished with the phrase, "Irish need not apply."

"Shure then, and purroud I am of it," said Peggy, thickening her natural brogue for Aunt Lucy's benefit.

"Insolent girl," hissed Mrs. Pleet, clenching her fists. "You can be dismissed tomorrow."

"I fear not," Lady Sibilla interjected in her low, expressive voice. "Peggy is part of the family. She has been my friend and companion since my father brought her to Partridge Park when we were both seven. He promised her she could come to London with me when I came out, and so she has."

"Ridiculous!" stated Aunt Lucy, "Who is she?"

"My mother was Bridget Banks. She died when I was five," Peggy recited slowly, "and then I was raised at Corroughsmere until the Earrul died. When the present Earrul came to Ireland for the funeral, he took me back with him."

"I daresay she'll be running off to Mass and all of those other heathenish Popish rituals," Aunt Lucy speculated grimly.

"Sunday's always been my day off," Peggy said quickly, bobbing and adding, "Mrs. Pleet."

"Speak when spoken to," snapped Aunt Lucy. "Absolutely preposterous! A day off every week! Unheard of! You may have every fourth Thursday afternoon. No more. And you will stay under the condition that you remain upstairs acting as lady's maid to Miss Sibilla and Miss Sophia, but you are never, I repeat, never, to be found on the drawing room floor. I have not the slightest notion why my poor sister would allow her husband to bully her into granting such privileges to a mere serving girl, but such goings-on will not occur in my household. You are dismissed, Margaret—I assume your Christian name is Margaret?" Peggy nodded warily. "You will find Lily in the kitchen, and she will show you to a room."

Having heard these edicts in grim silence, Peggy marched briskly towards the door, a set stubborn look to her mouth, and the retriever, Slow, stumbling along after her rapid feet.

"Say 'Good night, Mrs. Pleet' when you leave the room!" commanded Aunt Lucy.

"Good night, Mrs. Pleet," mumbled Peggy, bending down and repeating more clearly, "Good night, Slow, honey." Then with a snap of her head which set all of her dark curls bouncing, she went out, slamming the door behind her, before Aunt Lucy could frame a retort.

The favouritism shown to Slow recalled to Mrs. Pleet's mind another order of business.

"These creatures!" she said distastefully. "Surely you do not propose to inflict these beasts upon my household!"

The retriever, sent away by Peggy, had returned to Sibilla's side, and she put a protective hand on his head as she responded to her aunt. "These are my pets, and I am responsible for their welfare. Let me assure you, they will give you no trouble."

"Certainly not," said Aunt Lucy briskly, "as they will be confined to the garden. Fortunately, there is a small one behind the house. I don't hold with this nonsense of letting animals have the run of a human habitation. As for that"—she pointed at Marmalade, who was sitting calmly at Sophy's side—"we may have a need for him. I would not be surprised to learn that the house is infested with mice; it seems to have gone to complete rack and ruin. But keep it out of my sight and away from visitors."

With an abrupt clap of her plump hands, Aunt Lucy finished with that subject and turned to her second objective, assuming an air of affability which startled both sisters. She flopped her great bulk down upon one of the couches, sighed deeply, and indicated with a wave of her hand that the girls were to follow suit. Sibilla settled into her previous seat, while Sophy sat rigidly at the edge of a fragile chair.

"Tell me the news," Aunt Lucy said confidingly. "I have not had the opportunity to write to Maria for such a long time. How is your dear mother's health?"

"Still poorly," Sibilla replied slowly, measuring her words. "She remains confined to her bed, as she has been for the past ten years, although the doctors can find nothing wrong. She is not in pain, but weak and tires very easily." Secretly, Sibilla had decided that her mother had given up on life after having tried for some fifteen years to provide an heir to the Earldom and succeeding only in producing seven healthy daughters, while her two sons were born sickly and died infants. But this was a theory she shared only with Peggy.

"I see," Aunt Lucy said complacently, nodding her head. "And the Earl? Still having trouble with his properties, I imagine?"

"Well, the crops have been bad lately," Sibilla responded, in the same low, careful voice, "and then what with the labourers asking for higher wages and the tenants complaining of high rents, he has a difficult time of it."

"Yes, we all know about the disgraceful complaints of the lower classes," said Aunt Lucy grimly, "who are allowed to form secret societies and run rampant about the countryside destroying other people's private property."

Sibilla opened her mouth, as if about to respond to this, and closed it again.

"And your sisters," Aunt Lucy continued her interrogation. "It seems to me the eldest married a soldier."

"Charlotte," Sibilla replied. "She married Major Dudley Garlinghouse of the Horse Guards during her first Season. They live in London."

"Your mother was quite distressed about that," Mrs. Pleet said with satisfaction. "Penniless, isn't he?"

"He has no immediate prospects," Sibilla admitted grudgingly.

"But he's so very handsome," Sophy interjected eagerly. "They fell in love at first sight, didn't they, Sibil?"

"Humph!" Aunt Lucy commented, and squelched Sophy's sentimental notions with one sharp glance.

"And then the next married a poor parson, did she not?" Aunt Lucy added ruthlessly.

"Oh, but Amy is so very happy," Sophy eagerly offered, forgetting momentarily her aunt's views on romance. "She met

191

him at a missionary meeting during her first Season and our parents wouldn't hear of such a match, so he did not even declare his feelings. Imagine Amy living through a whole year without knowing that he loved her! Then, the next Season, Nell accepted Lord Cloudsleigh, and since she had made such a good match, my parents gave permission to Amy and Reverend Brittle. They live with their eight—or is it seven children, Sibil?—in a poor section of London and do good deeds for their neighbours."

"Rubbish!" was Aunt Lucy's opinion. "Suffering and poverty are nature's admonitions to the undeserving. Misguided attempts at benevolence have always been more productive of evil than good."

Sophy subsided once more.

"I did hear of Nell—Eleanor's—marriage to Lord Cloudsleigh, that would be Baron Cloudsleigh, whose father is the Marquis of Merryfield with estates in Cambridgeshire." Mrs. Pleet shook her head sadly. "Why Nell—Eleanor's—husband is old enough to be her father, and his son by his first marriage must have been nearly her age when the wedding took place."

"He was twelve," Sibilla said stubbornly. "We met him at the wedding; he had been away at school for some time."

"No good can come of such a marriage," commented Aunt Lucy cheerfully. "It's no wonder that I hear Eleanor flirts shamelessly with all the young swells about town. But I do not understand why her husband permits it."

Both sisters looked at each other fiercely, but could not deny the charges their aunt had brought.

"Whatever happened to the next two?" asked Aunt Lucy blithely. "I heard nothing after Eleanor's marriage."

Sibilla and Sophy glanced at each other again.

"Effie decided to stay at home and never marry," Sibilla said cautiously. "Nell brought her out for her Season, but Effie found that the social whirl was not to her liking and returned home in the middle of it and has been there ever since." There was much more she could add: Effie's abrupt arrival in the middle of the night, her declaration that she would never return to London, her stubborn refusal to speak about Nell's house and Nell's hospitality, her denials that a specific incident might have caused her sudden flight. No one yet knew the reason for Effie's return, but Sibilla suspected an unhappy love affair, for Effie was listless and sat gazing out of windows for the first several months, until she put on her sturdy shoes and took to tramping about the countryside and attending church services regularly.

"Effie?" inquired Aunt Lucy brightly. "That would be Euphemia, the fourth. But what of the fifth girl, Catherine, or Kitty, I believe your mother called her."

"Kitty!" The very name had a peculiar and immediate effect upon the two sisters. Sophy flushed and sighed, remembering her favourite sister, indeed the favourite of the family, laughing, loving Kitty. And Sibilla stiffened. As the unofficial spokesman for the Merrell family, she found it difficult to frame her reply. At last she decided that blunt honesty was the best approach and thus, bracing herself, she said,

"Kitty vanished in the middle of her first London Season!"

www.ingramcontent.com/pod-product-compliance
Lightning Source LLC
Chambersburg PA
CBHW020622180626
46810CB00007B/2895